sometimes i lie
and sometimes i don't

Nadja Spiegel

sometimes i lie
and sometimes i don't

stories

Translated from the German
by Rachel McNicholl

DALKEY ARCHIVE PRESS

Originally published in German as *manchmal lüge ich und manchmal nicht*
by Skarabæus Verlag, 2011. © 2011 by Skarabæus Verlag

Translation copyright © 2015 Rachel McNicholl
"death and ophelia" was first translated by Rachel McNicholl for "Words on the
Street: European Literature Night," Dublin, 2012. The translation was first published
in *The Stinging Fly*, issue 25, vol. 2, summer 2013.
First edition, 2015

LIBRARY OF CONGRESS CATALOGING-IN-PUBLICATION DATA

Spiegel, Nadja, 1992- author.
[Short stories Selections. English]
Sometimes I lie and sometimes I don't / by Nadja Spiegel ; Translated by Rachel McNicholl.
-- First edition.
    pages cm
Summary: Love, injury, deception, uncertainty, and self-sacrifice: debut author Nadja Spiegel is
hardly the first person to write about these things, but the way she has written about them is in-
comparable. Constructing virtuoso depictions of life in a style that lets them get right under your
skin, Spiegel's precise, brittle, seemingly straightforward prose paints a vibrant picture of human
compromise and cooperation with both humor and restraint. Bittersweet, made up of just a few
simple strokes, these stories herald the arrival of an important new voice in European literature.
-- Provided by publisher
Originally published in 2011, under title: Manchmal lüge ich und manchmal nicht.
ISBN 978-1-62897-062-3 (pbk. : alk. paper)
I. McNicholl, Rachel, translator. II. Title.

PT2721.P48A6 2015
833'.92--dc23

2015016434

This book was partially funded by a grant by the Illinois Arts Council, a state agency.

 BUNDESKANZLERAMT ■ ÖSTERREICH

The translation of this book was supported by the Austrian Federal Ministry of Education,
Arts and Culture. This book received financial assistance from the Arts Council of Ireland.
The publisher acknowledges the financial assistance of Ireland Literature Exchange
(translation fund), Dublin, Ireland.
www.irelandliterature.com
info@irelandliterature.com

www.dalkeyarchive.com
Victoria, TX / London / Dublin

Cover: typography & layout by Arnold Kotra
composition by Jeffrey Higgins

Typesetting: Mikhail Iliatov

Printed on permanent/durable acid-free paper

contents

meta plays the violin

The fiddle-leaf fig belongs to the mulberry family. *It needs a lot of light*, I say. I say it softly and airily, the way I imagine a voice made of light. Meta slides to the edge of the bed, her cold toes brushing my thigh; she's off to clean her teeth, she says. I let my fingers circle the warm space where Meta just lay.

Meta does not have green fingers. Meta plays the violin.

This is how it was with Meta and me: on my first night in the flat-share I banged my nose when I walked into the glass door between the living room and the bedroom; later, I banged my knee when I stumbled over Meta's violin in the dark, between the bedroom and the living room. My nose cracked, the violin split in two; Meta hung the nicer half on the door of her room.

Meta does not have green fingers. Meta plays the violin. Meta cannot heat berries in a saucepan without burning them. Meta is from Ukraine. Meta's hands are so cold in the morning and in the middle of the day that I imagine they must be blue at night. Meta's songs have a Volga sound about them.

There are two Metas. That's what I thought the first month, when I was getting to know Meta.

There's the Meta who chews her pen until it splits and her mouth turns blue, her fingers too. Who sits in the back row, left corner, and is a sponge. And then there's the Meta who drinks too much beer and says she wants to be a violinist and then claps her hand to her mouth and shouts *Blinddeaf-*

dumb, is that what we are, is that what we are, Anne, is it?

On evenings like that, Meta puts on Albinoni or Vivaldi to keep her ears shut. Then Meta is a wall.

Meta and I are known as the two of them: Meta being the one with the violin and the broken German, me being the other who counts the pages of books before buying them and comes from Austria and talks that way too. It was always better to be the one than the other, because the one was the child prodigy and the other only someone who counts the pages of books before buying them and comes from Austria and talks that way too.

When I say *I'm not jealous*, Meta smiles. I like it when Meta smiles, because then I can split Meta open and pick the nicer side and hang it on the door. At first I was ashamed for having this thought. When Meta smiles, she is naked. Meta does not look nice naked.

Sometimes Meta and I are also the three of them: that's when Paul is there, which is on Saturdays, and on Saturdays, Meta and Paul are too far from me and too close to each other. Then I can still see Paul in Meta's face the next day, when she says *I'm off for a shower* and I put my ear to the floor the better to hear her footsteps in the bathroom.

Paul is there pretty much every Saturday. If there's an exception to the pretty much, then the name is not Paul but Michael or Joachim; then Meta's high bed creaks as she climbs down the ladder. Her bare feet on the floor sound like puddles and cold. On Saturdays like that, Meta is a wall; a very thin wall, the way she's propped against the windowsill in the morning wearing only a T-shirt and panties that could have *big bang* written on them — more like a curtain, almost, the way she turns to me and says *He's gone already, will I put on Vivaldi?*, and looks like winter. I picture Paul or Michael or Joachim laughing when they see Meta's panties, and I turn red.

If I keep very still and count my breaths, Meta eventually stops talking too and the waves of our breathing wash in and out together. Then Meta forgets who she is. I know this; she told me. *When I listen to Vivaldi*, she said, *I know who I am, and when I listen to you breathing, I forget who I am.*

Meta wears little summer dresses and leather jackets on stage, and her music sounds like summer and leather too, like snow and toothpaste. Meta kissed me once; it was at midnight and after *Blinddeafdumb, is that what we are, is that what we are, Anne, is it?* We were sitting on the sofa, the leather upholstery squeaking, when she slid closer to me; her hand on my shoulder was like snow and her face so close I could no longer see her freckles. Meta's tongue tasted like peppermint.

You and your music, you're one and the same, I sometimes say. Meta doesn't smile then but puts quizzical fingers to her lips, and it's like when you ride over a pothole in a stuffy, airless coach.

Meta says she thinks it's her accent that men fall for. I say nothing and flip through the images I have of Meta's men. One is of Meta at the dinner table, sitting on someone's lap, holding a glass of red wine, laughing, her curls bouncing; a second one, later, is of Meta alone at the dinner table, humming Albinoni and keeping time with her feet.

In another image, the doorbell rings, Meta's taking a bath

and I'm stewing fruit. Meta shouts *Open the door and send him in to me in the bathroom!,* and the someone I'm meant to send to the bathroom looks at my dirty apron and my red cheeks and raises his eyebrows.

Then an image immediately afterwards in which I say he should head for the bathroom, and he grins, making me think all at once of vodka, sherry and brandy and of Meta pulling a face whenever she drinks whiskey, and sighing with satisfaction a moment later.

Fiddle-leaf figs belong to the mulberry family. I gave Meta the plant for her birthday. It spent three weeks on her bedside table and the fourth beside the rubbish bin behind Study Block 5. *Fiddle-leaf figs need a lot of light*, I had said, and Meta had said *Yes.*

When Meta speaks, it sounds like bogs and bark, not like light.

Sometimes Meta gives me a hand with the cooking, or at least that's what she calls it. *I'll help with the cooking, I'll give you a hand today*, she says, and sits on the worktop and watches me cry while I chop onions, and later, when I'm stirring things or turning them over, she comes up behind me, rests her chin on my shoulder and plants a kiss on the nape of my neck. That's when I'd like to tell her that she's doing lots of things, but helping isn't one of them. Instead I say *Stop that, I smell of cooking oil and onions.*

When Meta and I introduce ourselves, Meta says *My name is Meta, I'm a violinist, and this is Anne; Anne cooks and has houseplants.* Then the other person laughs — with Meta and at me.

That's me. Anne. Anne cooks. Anne has houseplants. And Anne is not jealous.

Paul—why not Paul? asked Meta and I said, *When you kiss Paul, on Saturdays sometimes, do you ask him that too*: Anne—why not Anne? *Do you?* Meta laughed then and gave me a thump on the arm. *We're only having a bit of fun. You know there's nothing to it, nothing serious.* The first time she said that, a shadow fell across her face that hid only the eye that was winking. *But I don't think it's funny*, I said softly, *I think it's serious.*

When Paul comes on Saturdays, he hugs me just a little too long—when he leaves, when he arrives and sometimes in between too. When Paul drinks from my glass he is more of a stranger to me than when he kisses Meta later, and when Paul says *Hi* it matches his too-wide T-shirts and his size 44 shoes.

That was during my first year here, when Paul wasn't kissing Meta yet but used to keep my hair out of my face while I cooked for the three of us, and the way he looked at me sometimes made me wonder if Paul's tongue tasted like peppermint too. *It doesn't*, Meta tells me. She says Paul's tongue tastes like lovage, and that it's all a bit like sawdust with him; or rather I put it to her, *I imagine it must be a bit like sawdust with Paul, is it?*, and Meta sat on the edge of the bed pulling her tights on, clicked her tongue and said, *Yes, maybe it is.*

Paul never kissed me. But once, when all three of us were standing at the apartment door one morning, Meta in nothing but her panties and me in one of my oversized nighties, Paul said *I wish you'd let me kiss you some time.* I went red and looked at Paul's shoes. Later, when the door was closed, Meta's face looked all cracked up. *Is something wrong?* I asked, and she said No but it sounded like Yes.

Meta is at her most beautiful when she emerges from the bathroom after a shower, a towel wrapped around her head, a few strands of hair usually escaping, and her nipples showing under her cami top. Meta is at her most beautiful when I no longer know where to touch her or whether she is touchable at all. Perhaps that's when everyone is at their most beautiful.

Whenever Meta answers questions at our seminars, she speaks so fast and with so many cross-references, footnotes and technical terms that no one can understand what she's saying. When she's finished, the professor puts on an expression for a minute as if he had recorded Meta and needs to replay her sentences slowly; then for five minutes he puts on another expression as if to say *I understand*, but the words he says during these five minutes show no understanding at all.

Meta speaks as if she has read all the scholarly works one can possibly read about music. Meta says *You must make sure you've read everything, then you'll get to just play the violin.* And *You must speak and write as quick as you can in an exam, so that afterwards you'll have more time to practise.* When the lecturer says, *You may sit down. Well done*, Meta tosses her hair and winks over her shoulder at the rest of the room, looking like she's mouthing *Pff* or *Tss*. Everyone laughs then, and I look at Paul, who's chewing his bottom lip and making a face like Meta's a pain.

I'm Meta, I play the violin, Meta had said the time she introduced herself. It was a Saturday. I was sitting in the kitchen,

Paul was making coffee, and Meta stumbled in wearing only panties. *I'm Meta, I play the violin, and that's Paul, Paul is here on Saturdays to make coffee, and on Sundays he drives the ice resurfacer at the rink. Paul is a constant, right—you are, Paul, aren't you?* That's what she said, and she laughed, and her laughter roared just like her music, like the Volga, so loudly that I don't remember whether Paul laughed as well.

I wish you'd let me kiss you some time, Paul says, and he kisses Meta and I say nothing.

Footnote:

1.

a) Meta cannot heat berries in a saucepan without burning them. Meta is from Ukraine. Meta does not have green fingers. Meta's hands are blue.

b) Paul is there on Saturdays to make coffee, and on Sundays he drives the ice resurfacer at the rink.

c) Anne cooks and has houseplants.

2.

a) What everyone knows: Meta plays the violin.

b) What no one knows:

death and ophelia

I

Does anyone open the car door for a lady these days, girls and boys, says Ophelia, shaking her head and forgetting to add the question mark.

She covers her eyes with her hands. The skin on Ophelia's hands is old, old on her wrists too, her fingers, her face— Ophelia's skin is old all over. You could cut her skin open and peel it off, undress Ophelia, fold her skin and hang it on a clothes horse.

Ophelia's skin is old. Not Ophelia.

Does anyone write letters at all these days, boys and girls, says Ophelia, sitting in her armchair and sliding her hands under her thighs. *It's my back*, she says; *the base of my spine*, she says.

Ophelia has a lot of whys and becauses, and sometimes when we go to see Ophelia—we just say *going to see Ophelia* because, according to her, "going to the old folks' home" *has a bit of death about it*— then Ophelia has lots of once-uponatimes too, and smiles a lot, and her smile looks like washing fresh out of the tumble-drier.

In the top drawer of her bedside table Ophelia keeps sweets; they're like scratchy marbles in your mouth, and they suit Ophelia's voice, the way it rewinds and spools and sometimes stalls when she talks about the past. Ever so slowly Ophelia coils a *backthen* and a *wheniwasyourage* around her neck until every word is a rope.

Ophelia likes us because she has someone to listen to her; she doesn't remember our faces or our names.

II

Girls and boys, boys and girls, says Ophelia.

In my day we were always going out; we went dancing in short skirts and high heels, and the men's eyes would follow us, and really Tom was the only one I was interested in, with those blue eyes, that look that would make you think of Paris, says Ophelia, but the look in her eyes doesn't make you think of Paris, more of a vase teetering on the edge of the table.

Ophelia talks and tells stories and sighs often in between. We laugh a lot so that Ophelia can feel amusing, ask a lot of questions so that Ophelia can feel interesting, and we're there so that Ophelia can feel younger. Ophelia: we say it a lot, it's a nice name; it doesn't suit the woman who paces up and down in her room and straightens out the fringes of her rug with a big wide comb. Ophelia: it goes with puckered red lips, giggly glasses of champagne, smudged kisses on cheeks. Ophelia sounds like curtain calls and bows and glances tossed over your shoulder.

I was never in theatre, children, no, says Ophelia and laughs; she has forgotten how to laugh — it tumbles awkwardly from her lips, falls onto the rug with a muffled thud. We nod, but that doesn't change anything; for us, Ophelia has always been on stage, and only in lead roles. She was a singer, she was in the opera. That's how it is, that's how Ophelia is. For us.

III

When Ophelia walks from her room to the lounge, it looks a bit like an aubergine with two forks for legs. Ophelia's breathing is dry; when Ophelia's asleep, one of us says *Death is coming. It creeps into the body and creeps out again. That's okay for a while, but when the while is up, the body is just a hollow body, and death creeps in and lies down to sleep*, and we nod and hold Ophelia's hands, stroke her cheeks; the skin there looks like it was left behind by mistake. If we're there in the evenings and Ophelia's asleep, it feels a bit like in church when you accidentally drop the car keys you've been fidgeting away with.

We talk about death because it's part of it all, the same way we often talk about feet. Because one of us knows that *People don't talk nearly enough about feet; that isn't right; we all end at our feet, don't we?* And so we talk about death and we talk about Ophelia too, and in between we put ands, and before that a few ifs and whens and us.

Ophelia's breathing is an inflatable ball that's gone a bit flat, and when she talks she stretches her voice around the stories until it tears. Ophelia might die soon, we know that. We're there so that only Ophelia's body will die in this white bed in this white room and not Ophelia.

IV

Ophelia only tells us the stories that make us blush for her; she likes our red cheeks; she reaches out to touch them; *Beetroot children*, she says, and we laugh so that Ophelia can laugh too.

Ophelia tells stories and we sit on the edge of her bed, say *Yes, Ophelia*, and pull the covers up to her chin so that our hands have something to do when she talks about Tom's hands that are so like his mouth, soft and sure. We fix her sheets, tucking them in tight so that we don't have to look at each other when Ophelia talks about Tom's mouth, Tom's mouth between her legs. We blush. For ourselves, maybe, but mainly for Ophelia, lying there all wrinkles and folds.

What happened with Tom in the end? one of us asks and Ophelia says: *Jan.* We say *Who's Jan?*, and Ophelia says: *Josef and Anton and Bernd.* And then Ophelia tells us about *JosefAntonBernd* sitting naked on the kitchen table and herself in her underwear washing last night's dishes and *JosefAntonBernd* laughing. In Ophelia's stories, people are always beautiful.

V

It's Sunday and Ophelia's mouth is full of flour. One of us found her in the afternoon, on the rug, with a comb. *Heart attack*, the one of us says and we nod. Death. Ophelia. In between an and.

It's like that feeling in church when you accidentally drop the car keys you've been fidgeting away with. It feels like breathing in and trembling and waiting and waiting until someone says you can breathe out. And that's how it should be.

Ophelia, we say, and lie down on the rug with our feet sole to sole.

how it is

The anthracite night has wrapped itself round the house, no more than a gentle whisper.

Hey, she says, sitting on the end of the bed, tucking her feet under the covers; she has cold toes.

Hey, you awake? I turn on the light; the glare hurts my eyes. She blinks. It's four in the morning.

What's up? My voice sounds like birch bark, rough. If I peel it, it would sound like: Go away.

They said I should apply, you know; they said I might make it, they really did, so I put in an application — yesterday, actually.

She tucks her hair behind her ear. Her words sound dead; they rasp at the air until it is so thin I can only breathe through my mouth.

Right, I say, because I can't think of anything else. *Right*, and then *Go to sleep.* She laughs, gets up, and her footsteps on the wooden floor are light and dainty — like a pigeon's, I imagine. In the doorway she turns back, smiling an apologetic smile, the kind she grants the audience when she bows at the end of a performance: *What do you think?* I shrug my shoulders and turn to face the wall.

The door closes gently, just a quiet click, and I say *Of course they'll accept you.* What I don't say is: *I don't want them to accept you.*

I saw my sister on stage twice: a first time and a last time. The first time was with my mother. She curled her lip when my sister took a bow at the end; she didn't clap; she didn't bring flowers or chocolates either, or a card that might have said:

I'm very proud of you. My mother is not a proud woman. My sister calls her domineering, bitter, and simple-minded.

The last time was without my mother. *We can't afford to go*, she said; I hadn't even asked, but she said it anyway. It was a cold night, the living room window was open, *Tatort* was on TV. I can't remember what the crime was; all I remember is the main characters' faces. *We can't afford to go, you know that; of course you know.* I do know, but I also know there are complimentary tickets for family members; my sister gave me two. She didn't say *For Mother and you*; she said *For you*.

I went to the Friday evening show with two tickets all to myself. It was Schiller's *The Robbers*. I forget what role my sister played; she was on stage three times, and three times she granted the audience polite, apologetic smiles, the cardboard kind you can tear up, like I did with the second ticket.

Did you like it? my sister asked. She came to my room at five in the morning, cigarette smoke lingering in her hair, alcohol on her breath and someone's cheap after-shave on her neck. I said *Yes* and couldn't remember anything about the play, only about *No*.

My sister is an actor.

I'm the only one who says that. My mother says nothing; my mother does not discuss acting or the fact that she has two daughters.

I'd like to study acting, says my sister, and she needs to go abroad, *because the courses are better there*, she says.

My mother shrugs her shoulders, and if we're watching *Tatort* and my sister isn't at home, she says, *Such a load of nonsense. She's nowhere near good enough.*

My mother is not a happy woman. She says so herself.

My mother is a woman who has decided to be unhappy; my mother wears her unhappiness with a stubbornness bordering on self-abasement.

In the mornings, my mother works in the bakery round the corner, where they put your bread rolls in yellow paper bags, and the coffee and hot chocolate in chipped white cups with broken handles.

On Sundays I have breakfast in the bakery during my mother's shift, because it doesn't cost us anything. My mother always puts an extra pat of butter on the wooden board that smells of soap and coffee. I watch her talking to the customers with tight lips and tight words; her hand shakes when she puts the coffee down on the table, and she generally forgets the milk and sugar—at least that's what the customers say; they lean against the counter and put on a pained smile before they say: *When you have a chance, could I have a little milk and sugar, please; you must have forgotten it.* My mother never forgets the milk and sugar; my mother just doesn't understand that there are people out there who do not drink their coffee black.

Sometimes I help out in the cafe on Saturdays and Sundays, when my mother has back trouble or migraine. This happens three Saturdays out of four. Then I put on her red bib, which is too tight across my chest and too loose around my middle; smile my sister's smile, which I rehearse in the morning in front of the mirror; and serve the coffee, always with milk and sugar, even if the customers order black coffee.

Sometimes my sister drops in, on days she knows my mother is at home in bed, sleeping and cursing and never saying

Thanks when I take her shift. My sister always sits at the same table, the one in the corner by the window, orders a cappuccino and asks me to join her just for five minutes; and so we sit across from each other just for five minutes. Her gaze shifts from my hair to my eyes to my hands and back again; she tells me I should wear warmer, darker colours like burgundy, and asks me to go out with her in the evening, after rehearsals.

Sometimes she asks — before we get to the bit where she invites me out — what I want to do with my life, but mostly she asks me that later, and when I shrug my shoulders she curses my mother, says she's planning to leave soon anyway, that I can move in with her then, and in the same instant she props her chin on her hands and asks me would I not like to repeat the *Abitur*, would I not like to go to university. But she doesn't let me answer; she tacks her dreams, her visions, her future onto each of her questions. Sometimes I wonder if what she'd really like is for me to be like her; to be able to tell her what I want to do when I'm older; for me to get my *Abitur* and go to university, abroad, somewhere far away from my mother.

The other days of the week, from Monday to Friday, I work in the kitchens at Die Sonne, up in the forest. The red paint is peeling off the chairs on the terrace; the plates have gold rims. I told my mother: *I like it a lot.* She shook her head and said: *A job is not something you like a lot. A job is a job; and jobs are no fun.*

I told my sister: *I like it a lot.* She slid the cookie that came with her cappuccino between her teeth and mumbled: *You like it? So that's the kind of thing you like, then.*

I don't know whether I like it a lot, or simply like it, or

whether I like it at all.

The food in Die Sonne is edible, just about, the people are okay, just about, and Die Sonne has two stars, also just about.

I get a half-hour for lunch every day, and I sit on one of the wooden benches out the back with the other staff; there are no tables here, no need for them either. Most folk don't eat anything anyway, just smoke and look around blankly, and the ones who do eat balance their plates on their knees, guiding forks to their mouths in slow motion and chewing in slow motion too.

I said to my mother: *It's quiet more than anything else.* She gave me an off-the-wall kind of look — a little off to the right, as if she wasn't looking at me at all — and said: *What do you care? Be glad that it's quiet.*

I said to my sister: *More than anything else, I like the quiet.* She looked me straight in the eyes and I didn't know where to look; I studied her eyes, her nose, her lips. She said: *You like that? The quiet?*

In Die Sonne the walls converge on each other and the stillness between them drowns out the kitchen noises. When I've done all my work, I have to shape the words in my mouth a few times, roll them into balls with my tongue and polish them with my teeth before I throw them into the room. *I'm finished. Anything else I can do?*

When I applied to Die Sonne I said *I can't cook*, and Frau Gretel laughed and said *Aha*; next day the phone rang at seven in the morning. Frau Gretel didn't say who she was but I recognised her voice, the kind that sounds soured with a dash of lemon. *You can start on Thursday, from eight 'til six, Monday to Friday. No overtime pay.*

After my first day at work I realised Die Sonne has no

need of apprentices who can cook. From eight in the morning until six in the evening I peel potatoes, wash lettuce, boil quails' eggs, slice peppers and carrots for mixed salads, stir instant sauces, shell broad beans and clean chanterelles. For another two hours, until eight, when the bus heads back to the valley, I wait for the bus to take me back down the valley.

I've only been out a few times with my workmates; I can count the number of times on two hands, maybe even on one. I don't really go in for talk for the sake of talking.

Today the bus was ten minutes late. It's only a few steps from the bus stop to our house. My mother is already there when I get home. There's a smell of burnt milk and sugar. *We're having potatoes for dinner*, says my mother. The table is already set, knives and forks in the wrong places; I put my shoes side by side in the hall closet; my mother's shoes lie higgledy-piggledy on the floor; I put them away neatly; then I sit down at the kitchen table. The potatoes are still hard in the middle. The milk pudding tastes of sugar and burnt milk and slightly of detergent.

Is it good? she asks. Her gaze burrows under my skin and lodges there.

I shrug my shoulders and say *Yes*.

You could do the odd bit of cooking too — what else are you an apprentice chef for, ha?

Later, we watch the *Tatort* from the week before last. Mother shoves the cassette into the VCR. She has to go down on her knees to do it; I help her up; she doesn't smile back; she plants her hands on her back, and her lower lip trembles. *Do I look that old — like I need your help?* I shake my head.

My mother answers the ringing phone. She says *Elisabeth Gartner*, then she says nothing, just nods. *For you.* She hands me the phone and leaves the room. It's not for me; it's my sister.

What would you say if I had a place at college in America, and an apartment, and if I asked you to move in with me? Her voice is smiling, laughing; I cock my head and run my tongue over my teeth.

They've accepted you.

Yeah, the letter came today. I'd been expecting it last week, so I figured they mustn't want me, but today— they really have accepted me.

Sounds like they have, all right. I bite my tongue, wind the telephone cable round my fingers.

Aren't you pleased?

My mother's footsteps outside the living room, the creak of the door, her slow, shuffling steps. She sits down beside me but doesn't look at me; she looks at the television.

Yeah . . . yes, of course. Congratulations.

Thanks.

The silence that follows her *Thanks* feels like the stillness in Die Sonne or the quaky feeling in my stomach when my sister asks me yet again what I want to do when I'm older, or right now, or at all. My mother is breathing loudly; she always does that when she's concentrating on her inhaling and exhaling. I glance at her out of the corner of my eye; she's reaching for the remote control.

Hey, we were watching Tatort. Mother wants to go back to it now. I hang up before my sister can say anything.

She's going off to study in America, I say. My mother turns her head towards me, says, *Aha*, and *It's what she wanted, isn't it.*

Then she turns the TV on. I have forgotten the plot of this *Tatort* from the week before last, and I still don't get who the murderer is in the end. Then I go to bed.

My sister is an actor.

I'm the only one who says that. My mother says nothing; she does not discuss acting or the fact that she has two daughters.

My sister is a happy woman.

I'm going to study acting, says my sister.

What would you say if I had an apartment in America and asked you to move in with me? She says that too.

It's Saturday, she's sitting at the corner table near the window, measuring two spoons of sugar into her coffee. We're sitting opposite each other, just for five minutes.

So, what would you say?

I brush my hair back, don't know where to look, look outside, say *Then I would say, that's very kind of you.*

Right. And what might that mean? That you'll come with me?

I look at her, shrug my shoulders.

Outside, she turns round once more and smiles through the shop window, a smile I don't recognise, and I smile her apologetic smile, the one she grants the audience when she bows at the end of a performance, the smile I've been practising before the mirror, the smile for customers.

No, is what I said. *No, I wouldn't like that.*

it's about crocodiles, stones and diving, says hannes

At night, Hannes folds variables in his head. During the day, he holds the variables in his hands like paper, holding them the way I wish he would hold me; and at night I hear the paper being creased, the edges being smoothed. Sometimes I drag my mouth over his skin then, and my lips split: when Hannes folds numbers in his head, he uses sandpaper.

Crocodiles eat stones so they can dive deeper, says Hannes, splaying his big book of mathematics across my knees.

When I'm at Hannes's place we often lie head to head on the carpet. We spend a lot of time lying down anyway, so that we don't tread on each other.

I am a number, Hannes says sometimes. The sometimes is on office days, which are grey days of which I have already assembled far too many visual images, and all the images are of Hannes's back. When I think of Hannes, I can only ever see him from behind or running his hand over his brow and through his hair. *I am a number*— Hannes says that a lot, and I count his steps to the study. The click of the door curls into the shell of my ear.

It was a birthday party; I can't remember whose. It was snowing outside and Hannes, propped in the doorframe, had only a thin shirt on; he was blowing cigarette smoke through his nose. Hannes didn't say hello straight away; first he just nodded his head, the way his hand might strike through an equation. He didn't say hello until after I had slipped on the icy pavement and cut my chin. *Hello there*, he laughed, and then *Let's get you back on your feet*.

Later, when I was sitting on the worktop near the kitchen sink and Hannes had made coffee, I burnt my tongue with the first mouthful. He asked what I did, in general. I said *Nothing in particular*. He laughed and ran his thumb along my cheek.

In the evenings, Hannes sometimes tries to find out what bit of me will bend. Those are mostly weekend evenings when I couldn't be bothered cooking and we have pasta with sauce from the jar.

I was always very straight, I said. Hannes laughs the kind of laugh that really means Yes.

I only asked Hannes once to help me with an assignment. His explanations came on stilts and collapsed just before they got to me; he said it was easy, that I was stupid, and he bounced tennis balls off the walls. *Work out what the damned x is*, he said later; his face was loud then, his voice too, and I breathed my head into a calm and empty state.

X is a variable which can describe any number. That is the only sentence I can remember from maths class.

Crocodiles eat stones so they can dive deeper, says Hannes.

On days with Hannes you can slit the bellies open and take out the stones. I put the stones in cardboard boxes under my bed, one for every month. Sometimes when Hannes says *I am a number,* with a face that looks like the plants in my room — like swamp or desert, nothing before, after or in between — then my bed is a quarry and I bang the stones randomly off each until I can play *Frère Jacques*. Hannes cannot fold variables if he's listening to music—he only cuts himself on the paper.

You smoke too much and you've been at it too long. I say that to Hannes frequently; he laughs back with a laugh like steel wool and blows smoke in my face. For Hannes I'd gladly be a variable or a cigarette. I wonder if that sentence would make him laugh too, or if he'd fling those words about the way he flings them when we fight. *You're boring. All you do is read stupid books—novels, that's all you read. And you don't even do that since we've been together. You're stupid, so you are. Stupid.*

I never did explain to Hannes that he ate into all my books; just into the corners at first, then into the lines, into the sentences. Now I only read in months when Hannes's *I am a number* fast-forwards and rewinds and I forget what his mouth looks like.

People addressed others as *Du* more than they should, Hannes had told me—or shouted, rather—on the dance floor; it was so loud in the disco I had to ask him twice, *What did you say?* Hannes is the kind of person who will suggest being on informal *Du* terms even though you've never used the formal *Sie* with each other. I like that but I don't say so. *Du*, Hannes said later, and I'd rather the scene had been: me on the dance floor, Hannes putting his hands on my hips, whispering in my ear, *Hallo, schönes Fräulein Sie.* But by then it was too late, I was already *Du*.

The arithmetic mean of two numbers is the sum of those numbers divided by two. If Hannes is Hannes, and Hannes equals one, and if I also equal one, and if the mean of one and one is one, and if one of us is between us—which of us has gone and which of us hasn't?

Buy yourself some decent tights, said Hannes, the time I invited him to dinner. The pasta was taking too long to cook—I was being impatient as usual; the tomato sauce was burning in the pan—I was being too patient as usual.

Hannes pointed at my thigh, at the hole in my tights, and touched his index finger to my skin; it fit perfectly into the rim of the hole. I chewed and swallowed, swallowed the spaghetti and the noises between my teeth.

Back then I still needed my own walls when I was with Hannes.

Now I cut the stones out of the days' bellies.

Hannes holds variables as if they were made of paper; he holds them the way I wish he would hold me. He could fold me in his head, in his belly, could crease me and smooth me and store me, all folded and smoothed, between yesterday and tomorrow.

Hannes only held me like paper once. He did not want to crease me or smooth me. He wanted to tear me up. The sound of screaming paper ate its way under my skin—ever since, I've been deaf under my skin, below my collar bone, towards my heart.

Hannes is the kind of person who offers the informal *Du* even to people he has never addressed as *Sie*. And the kind of person who revokes the *Du*, even from people he will never address as *Sie*.

Crocodiles eat stones so they can dive deeper, says Hannes. *Because that's what it's all about*, says Hannes. *Crocodiles, stones and diving.*

For Hannes, I would gladly have been a variable or a cigarette. It occurred to me some time later that it was all irrelevant anyway; I might as well have been a crocodile, a stone, or even water. That still wasn't what it was about.

It was I who wasn't relevant enough.

hunger

Dinner's ready, the mother shouts. She hides her hands among the dirty dishes and zips her lips in a line. The father's footsteps slap on the floor; his tongue slaps too against his teeth, and his teeth cut the bread, mince it into little pieces; grind and swallow. The father is a stork. The stork comes, sees, eats, leaves.

Mama, says the child, *Mama.* The child reaches its arms out to her, splays its fingers, grasps at thin, empty air.

Eat up, says the mother.

Breakfast, calls the mother. *Breakfast's ready.* She shoves her crying eyes under her sweater and paints a pair of big blue ones on her face; only then does she turn around. The father rustles his newspaper; the rustling swallows his footsteps. The father sits lopsided at the table; the bread in his mouth weighs too much in the wrong places. His mouth becomes long and pointy, turning into a beak. The beak drinks the coffee; it's hot and it burns the tip of the father's tongue. *Mama*, wails the child, *Hungry. Hungryhungryhungry.*

Here, says the mother. *Eat*, she says, her fingers tearing bread into pieces, shaping little squares, pushing the pieces between the child's lips.

Chew, she says, *chew.* And the child chews. Its eyes are rinsed plates on the draining board. The child keeps looking, at the mother's chin, at her cheek, her mouth, her nose. But the child does not look into the mother's eyes. The mother has cut the eyes out of her head.

The father's jawbones crunch, grind; the father's throat swallows, coughs.

What the child knows of the father: it knows the father's bird-mouth, knows how he eats too. And how he says *Ittastesnice*, how he and the mother nod, how they nod for the child.

Don't look at your father like that, says the mother. *You shouldn't stare at people, especially while they're eating. It's not done. People are not animals.*

The father nods, laughs. The child does not know the father's laugh; it sounds like a bird's squawking. The father opens his mouth wide when he laughs; mushy bread falls out onto the table and onto the plate. Then he gets up, then he leaves, then the front door bangs.

The last thing the child knows of the father: his gluey footsteps on the wooden floor at breakfast, lunch and dinner; his unsteady legs long after midnight, in the hallway, on the stairs, outside the child's bedroom.

The gaping distance between the mother and the child is the father's coming and going.

Eat up, says the mother. *Come on, eat up — or are you full.*

The child looks at its hands and arms. To rip them out is what it wants, to break them off at the wrists, cleave them at the elbows, hack off the fingers. Then it would file the palms into squares and yank the mother's lips and mouth wide open; it would shove in pieces of armhandelbow and squares of palm, it would stuff, squeeze, press and —

I'm full, says the child.

ginger light

*It seems only yesterday I used to believe
there was nothing under my skin but light.
If you cut me I could shine.*
(Billy Collins, "On Turning Ten")

There are two types of breathing, Milo told me once, *lunar
breathing and solar breathing.* That's why I loved him; because he always breathed out just as I breathed in. He didn't
steal my air, he gave it to me.

The first I saw of Milo was his back, with the ginger-shaped
birthmark half in the spotlight's pool of shadow. His hair
was a bit too short for me; I'd have liked to make it a little
longer in my picture, wilder too, but drawing nudes was like
painting by numbers, as if we artists weren't really entitled
to fill in the shapes.

It wasn't my first life-drawing class but it was the first
with a male model. My hand shook on the paper and my
strokes were too hard. I knew this, even without Madame
whispering into my ear on each of her rounds, *Mona, you
must draw softer lines.* But the way I saw Milo, as he stood
there directing his gaze straight through the wall as if it
wasn't there, Milo seemed made of steel.

You're drawing me too hard. His voice was deeper than I'd expected, its resonance a bit like muted light. *I know*, I said.
He didn't ask what I was doing there five hours too early;
instead he took off his clothes and stood in front of me. *It's*

your first time doing this, isn't it? I shook my head; my cheeks were burning; I pressed the backs of my hands to them. He smiled; he clearly didn't believe me. He reached for my hand and put it on his hip, nodding at my drawing. *I'm softer*, he said. I nodded; his skin felt hot to my touch, his smile etched its way into my fingertips. *It's not my first class — really*, I said; the smile continued its etching, invading a greater area, and I lowered my eyes to my drawing.

The third time we'd met like that, hours before the morning class, he'd invited me to his place for dinner. He opened the door with his elbow, a vegetable knife in one hand, a bowl of sliced peppers clamped under the other arm. *Hi*, he said. The apron suited him, though not enough; my eyes went no further than his collarbone. *You cook with so many colours*, I remarked, admiring them in the bowl.

In everything he does, an artist must see a subject he would like to paint, and — his voice was drowned out by the sizzle of oil in the pan.

How are you getting on with the life-drawing? he asked later. *I've done it before*, I said, my voice a bit unsteady from the red wine. *With a woman. Aha*, he went, *and does it bother you to be drawing me? I don't like drawing shapes without fill- ing them in*, I said, the red wine sloshing over the rim of my glass onto my blouse.

The sweater he lent me was too big; I tucked my hands into the sleeves and felt far too young for him. He tilted his head. *People with a Cupid's-bow upper lip are meant to be very sensitive, and good kissers; I'd really like to put that to the test.* He slid closer to me on the sofa; the leather uphol-stery squeaked. His lips were too soft and his kiss too hard, so I became quite confused when I was drawing his lips the following days. Madame reminded me to connect the lines more fluidly, to draw the contours more finely. I would have liked to tell her that my problem was trying to dissociate Milo's outer shell from Milo himself.

I hate white, said Milo, pointing at the sheet of paper on my lap. The sunlight was refracted off the balcony door. Milo's hair glowed reddish. *That's it, that's why I paint*, he said, *because all that white there has to go.* I shrugged my shoulders. *Light is white*, I said. I put my sketch of the roof across the street on the table and went for a shower.

When I was at Milo's, everything was light; that's why I only half-filled my sketchbook pages—to have a little piece of Milo on the other half. One Friday, I filled in a sketch of Milo with white crayon, but it still didn't feel like it was my picture. I waited for him in the living room until midnight. The curtains of the house across the street were drawn.

From the hip down, my nudes were blurry at first. It embar-rassed me to draw Milo, especially once I knew his skin felt too soft when I touched it and too hard when it touched me. *I don't know if I'd be able to paint you*, he had said that time, as his moan thrust into me. I tried to find some bit of him to hold because I felt the need to hold on to something, but it seemed as if nothing was left, just Milo and his light. And something slid asunder and slid back together again. *You are everywhere*, he said, *I couldn't paint you; you are too much.*

Let me paint you, he said later, *Naked, in the studio. Will you let me?* I couldn't say no, because I didn't want to. We set the lights a little too low, and I dabbed Milo's fragrance on my wrist so as not to feel quite so exposed. *How are you going to paint me*, I asked. *As if I'm behind bars*, he said. *I'll lock you within me and then I'll remove the bars, one by one.* I cleared my throat. Milo was too close, my clothes too far away. He put his hands on my arms, which were covering my breasts, and looked me in the eyes as he lowered my arms. *You are beautiful.* I stared at the floor and smelled my wrist. *An artist sees beauty in each of his subjects*, I said, and allowed Milo to arrange me on the sofa. He didn't smile while he was painting; he sucked in his lower lip and let me forget my nudity. The way he looked at me made my body irrelevant; it was an artist's gaze.

If you had been offered the chance, you'd have gone too, he wrote, in a letter that came on a Thursday three weeks later. Yes, if I had won a scholarship to art college, I'd have gone too; but I would have taken him with me, or at least asked if he would come. Two weeks later a parcel arrived, with a letter enclosed.

There was a lot of white, a little bit of gold in the corners, an area the colour and shape of three carnations, and lots of pink splashes, like pink peppercorns; across the top, a string of capers. I turned it the other way up. A lot of white, a little bit of gold in the corners, an area the colour and shape of three carnations, and lots of pink splashes, like pink peppercorns; across the bottom, a string of capers.

In the top right corner it said *I painted you exactly the way I see you, exactly the way you showed yourself to me.*

I will send the painting back to Milo.

I could not hang a painting in my living room that shows me naked.

a sliver of moon

Sometimes on those summer nights when it was too hot to sleep, when you tossed and turned every two minutes, drenched in sweat, and I asked every third time you turned *Hey, are you still awake* and you just snorted, then we would go hand in hand, in our bare feet and nightdresses, down to the lake. Its lapping calmed us, and we lay down naked, side by side on the jetty, and the cold, damp timber softened our skin while we waited. Waited for a sliver of moon to fall so we could drop it in a glass of water and never forget what water looks like when it is drowning in moonlight.

Your skin was pimply and so pale you could see through it; mine was sprinkled with freckles, and you loved counting them, though you always lost count and started over again, touching them as you counted; and you laughed at my goose bumps when your ice-cold fingers wandered from my face to my collar bone, from my breasts to my belly, and then you said *You are way more beautiful than me,* and we never counted to the end. Once you got to 135 but then you couldn't remember which ones you had already counted; another time you used a pen to put a dot on each freckle you had counted, but you ran out of steam at some stage, and Mama was really cross later at having a daughter covered in blue dots.

In sunset moments you leaned your head on my shoulder and we watched the lake bleed; I twisted your curls around my finger and we shared the fear that one day they might bleach out altogether from the sun; one time when you were mixing ketchup and mayonnaise, you suddenly said, *That's it — that's exactly what's going to happen to my hair,* and I said you were daft, a hair fetishist, but you didn't care, you just didn't go out when the sun was shining, and if you did, you lay in the shade wearing a loose-knit woolly cap. And you pulled a face when I asked if you'd like to play cards with us, because you never felt like it. I don't mean playing cards— you never felt like company.

In the afternoons, when the lake was teeming with children screeching and frolicking in the water, and women whose delight in their little treasures knew no bounds, you would go home and study angling books, which seemed pretty pointless to me, for every fish you caught—with your bare hands, standing ankle-deep in the water—got a kiss on its belly and was always thrown back. Once you held out a fish to me and laughed, *Kiss the fishy, Camille, go on, give it a kiss*, and I smelt brackish seaweed smells that night when my tongue ran over my lips like a slippery, cold surface.

When the sun's rays stopped bleaching the days, you said autumn was change and winter freedom, and the girls in school laughed at you and the boys thought you were weird, because they couldn't figure you out, I guess—not that I ever managed that, and we were sisters—and the boys would say *Well, if it isn't our little angling friend!* or the girls would say *What a pretty skirt, pet—is it one of your Granny's?* Sometimes I tried to stand up for you, if they were poking fun and saying *By the way, have you had sex yet?*, but in fact the only person who said that was Rudolf—my boyfriend Rudolf; the kind of cheeky handsome guy everyone thought was really cool. And Johannes, who would chime in *Ha ha, as if s h e would ever get off with someone. She'll die a virgin.* But the only reason he said anything was because he idolised Rudolf, and sometimes I caught him throwing an admiring look your way when you said nothing, just smiled, and your pink tooth gem sparkled in the sun. When you left them standing there, yes, that's when he threw you those looks, but only when no one was looking, except me. I saw those looks but I didn't think anything of it; I could not have imagined that things would escalate the way they did later.

How many times did I yell at you, shouting that you were a total embarrassment in your mustard colours and dowdy old-lady prints, and that you really should let your hair down now and again; it was easy, I could introduce you to a few nice guys; and I gently suggested that it couldn't be nice to be hated by everyone, that you were my sister, that things could be really great if you'd only fit in. But all you did was stare at the birthmark on my left nostril and reply with lines like *He who hates weakens himself and his whole being* or *Hatred always follows those who hate.*

Back then I wanted to patent solitude and take it away from you, but I never got a chance because you were solitary all the time — not always alone, but always solitary. Instead, I patented every summer night with you, every one of your smiles, and that feeling when you hugged me and I felt your breath on the back of my neck. But the patenting thing didn't really work the way I intended; I should have patented remembering instead, because remembering is a form of forgetting, but now it is too late and I no longer know whether your breath was cold or warm.

This morning, Michael wanted to know where I was during the night. You know, when I toss and turn in the bed in August, the whole house smells of damp wood and stale warmth, and my thoughts swell up and I heap too much sugar into my tea down in the kitchen. Outside, the moon splits into quarters and eighths in the crowns of the trees.

The summer we turned seven, you and I measured the grass in June. It came up to our hips, and we entered the height in the calendar, which we eventually threw away because the memory became more indelible than the reminder not to forget, and to this day I remember that the grass was exactly 51.3 cm high. But I never say any of this to Michael, nor will I, because it's none of his business anyway. I just stare at him. You would like his eyes — river-blue is what they are; I say *Smilla had a bad dream*, although that's a lie — I was the one who crept into Smilla's bed, squeezed her hand and said *Shhh, don't wake up, love*, when she asked what was wrong. And Michael says *I know you loved her back then, of course you did; and you still love her*, and I don't know whether it's true.

I stand up, tear a page out of the telephone directory and write with black marker on the densely printed page because I need to do the shopping, and Michael is annoying me, asking again, *What e x a c t l y was it that happened?*, and I'm already regretting that I needed someone to talk to; and before that, someone to love me. And Michael hasn't a clue what to make of the words that float around the room like empty soap bubbles, because the milky trail of his cigarette smoke distorts their meaning, and he asks *What are you doing there?* and I list off: *Coffee, sugar and three currant buns and a box of mini tampons*, because Smilla is afraid of those things, as she calls them, and thinks they're too big, and one evening she got into the bed beside me, kissed me on the cheek and said *What if I don't want to be a woman yet?* and I had to smile. Because she's so like me, because she was just as aghast when she saw the first red stain in her panties. *You would be so proud if you knew that her hair is red — not as red as yours, but dragon's-head-red just the same.*

Michael reaches for my hand and squeezes it, smiling; I like his smile; he says *You loved her*, and I say *Of course; she was my sister,* and he shakes his head, kisses my hand, *You know what I mean.* I turn my head away, because I wouldn't have thought he could read my absent look so well, and I stand up saying *I'm going to the lake now*; Michael doesn't wait for me to ask if he wants to come too; the door clicks shut. He understands me, and I don't know what that means.

When I go down to the lake alone, barefoot and naked but for my towel, I sometimes see a distorted moon dancing lightly on the ruffled surface, and I can't help thinking of you, of the veins showing through on the back of your hand, of your feet covered in mud. You always dived right down to the bottom and laughed at me because I said the pressure hurt my ears too much and I couldn't understand why that didn't happen to you. I see you standing in the ankle-deep water, and I see my laughing face; and one time you thought you were being particularly funny when you somersaulted into the lake and still hadn't surfaced a couple of minutes later — maybe it was less, but it seemed longer to me — and I was shouting *Stop, this is not funny*, and I jumped in after you, where I thought I'd seen you disappear, and I screamed and I wailed, and then a while later I heard laughter, and there you were on the shore. So I grabbed my towel and ran right past you, running away, though you were saying *Don't be mad, Camille, I was only having a laugh*. And so the second time, when the concentric circles grew fainter and fainter and only the wind scudded back and forth across the surface that had swallowed you, I just got up and left and thought *Yeah, right, having a laugh — what exactly do you mean by that?*

Later, when you slid into bed and asked *Are you still mad at me?* I stared at the bed clothes and replied *Why can't you be like everyone else? Why is it you can only be happy when it's just you and me?*, and the bed clothes rustled as you got up and came to sit beside me; you kissed my forehead and said *I love you, Camille*, and I turned to face you. You kissed me lightly on the lips and I said *We can't. It's not right*, and you kissed me again, longer, your tongue gliding over my closed lips; you smelled of melted earth and evening sun, of mandarins and rose oil, and your breath brushed my nose, my cheeks, my eyes, and we kept kissing until I pushed you away, and said *Johannes — you know the way he looks at you sometimes . . .* and you whispered *Don't be mad at me, but I can't do that kind of thing*, and you went for a shower, outside the house, and I heard the water slapping off the concrete tiles, and I wondered what you meant by *that kind of thing*, maybe me and Rudolf, or maybe you and Johannes; I could still feel your lips on mine, the slight saltiness of the lake in your hair; I thought of all those kisses under the trees, and I would gladly have flung my thoughts into the water so that the lake would wash them clean.

I don't know why, but we never spoke of it again, of whatever it was, of us; maybe they were already too precious, those few moments we had, like rare four-leaf clovers hiding in the meadows; and nobody in school knew that we went to the lake together; they would have laughed me out of it and asked what you looked like in a swimsuit, your skin must be as pale as anything, and Rudolf would have looked at me with disgust, because he's always asking me how I can possibly put up with a sister *like that*, and Johannes — well, Rudolf was always right in his eyes. These days I ask myself what he really thought, back then, and when I was with Rudolf in my room and he was undoing my bra, I thought of you, because I ought to have felt happy that he wanted me, and I loved him yet hated him because he was mean to you, although you didn't half ask for it, being as odd as two left feet, and then he kissed my navel and asked what the matter was, and I said *Nothing; this is really nice, with you.* And he said *I really can't believe you two are sisters.* He was wrong about that, because we were actually pretty alike, we just had different shells; yours was made of marble, mine of cardboard, but the kernel was the same — an apricot kernel, in fact, without the fleshy fruit.

I shrugged my shoulders when Rudolf started talking about you again, because I didn't know what to say; I never knew what I should say, in fact, including when we sat on the steps in school, Rudolf and Johannes and me and Margaret and Lisa. They giggled when Rudolf suddenly announced *It's time we taught that girl not to be such a fool. Seriously, someone has to make her be, like, normal.* Johannes gave him a strange look, and I asked *How do you mean?*, but Rudolf just grinned and winked at Johannes and said *I'll show you when the time is right*, and then he kissed me hard on the lips. The smell of cigarette smoke seeped into my gums. Smoking was cool in those days.

Sometimes, when I'm driving home to Mam and Dad—
who spend all their time in the swing seat in the garden
these days, looking at the pear trees that no longer bear
fruit—I crane my neck a little, tilting my head toward the
sun, and the angle of the light shifts, bathing my hair red.
Then I see your rooibos-red hair in the rear-view mirror,
and your face, and I twist my lips into a smile forever frac-
tured by you. Then I hear your feet on the jetty's rotting
timbers, feel the splashes after you plunge into the water,
and count the seconds until the water's surface is still again;
sometimes I get to 140, sometimes to 200. When I park in
front of the house and the gravel crunches under my feet
and I call out *Mam! Dad!*, my eyes are full of tears I hastily
brush away, for our parents' sake, but Mam notices anyway
and says *Come on, I'm your mother—do you think I won't notice if you're feeling down?*, and gives me a big hug, and Dad
doesn't know what to say. We watch old movies, just black
and white, because Mam can safely cry then, and say *Great
film, Camille, isn't it?*, and Dad doesn't need to say anything
because the actors have plenty to say, and I can stare absent-
ly out the window, down at the lake, where all the young-
sters jostle in the water. Then I turn away, because I can
feel Dad's gaze on my skin, out of the corners of his eyes;
he mutters some words and asks if I'd like a pear, the ones
from the supermarket aren't great but . . . He talks because
it's often good to talk, because the silence would be way too
loud, would suffocate us in this old house where the plaster
is crumbling like the masks we paint on our faces every day
in front of the mirror.

I never was able to patent that solitude, because it belongs to
everyone, not just to you, not just to me and you; like desire

or longing, which don't belong to anyone either. I can't remember Rudolf's girlfriend's name or her face (he got married since anyway); one time I bumped into him in the supermarket and he held up a hand and said *Hey,* just like he used to, as if time had stood still, and he asked how I was, his grey eyes anxious, and I said *I had a baby eight months ago,* and he said *Congratulations,* and his girlfriend wore a frozen smile and I wondered if she felt the way I used to feel back then, and Rudolf steered her off towards the checkout, his hand on her hip. I heard her whispering *Who was that, Rudolf?,* and him answering *That's a long story, love; it doesn't matter really,* and I turned those words, *doesn't matter really,* twisted and turned them left to right and inside out, but I just could not find the right side.

Just like the time I persuaded you to go down to the lake with me but didn't tell you that I'd invited him and Johannes along too, although in fact they had invited themselves when they said *Do you remember we said your sister could do with a lesson?,* and I promised to arrange it, the evening by the lake, because all I wanted was for you to act normal and for them to stop bad-mouthing you, and maybe for you and Johannes to get together, because I was scared, scared of what there was between you and me, and I thought a little company might bring a little contrast to your world of lake moments, of fish and seaweedy smells. But you didn't say a word the whole evening, not a single word, not even when Johannes grabbed your arm and you turned to face him, and he said mockingly *You really have quite a pretty face, you know . . . Well, little lady, what do you reckon, isn't it about time you had sex? Or do you want to die a virgin?* And Rudolf said you were seventeen now, for Christ's sake, there must be something wrong with you, and if you were waiting for

Prince Charming to come along, you could forget it. And I said nothing, nothing at all, my silent empty smile lost in the darkness.

I asked you again and again if I was a bad sister, but you never answered, except the one time you said *Do you mean because of what we do together?,* and later I didn't dare to ask, because I knew the answer already. I draw the moon on a sheet of squared paper and stick it to a stone which I then chuck into the water, but I don't wait for the water's surface to be still again; the lake kisses the red sky on the horizon and I run away because I always was a coward.

At home, I sit in the bath with a cup of rooibos tea; it's bitter and I don't like it; Smilla sits on the edge of the bath and wants to know what's wrong and whether I'm thinking of her. *Yes,* I say, and Smilla gives me a hug, says *I got the hang of the tampons today; it worked,* and that Tom wants to go out with her, that he said she had such gorgeous red hair. And I smile, say *That's wonderful, pet,* and when I can't help crying, Smilla cries with me, even though she knows nothing about guilt or how at some point we no longer wanted to be sisters but that wasn't possible because being sisters is a job for life, a birthmark on your heart; nor does she know that you decided at some point that it must be possible to sever the sister-bond. The weedy water was meant to break your birthmark down into tiny pieces.

You were lying naked by the lake and I sat down beside you. This was two days after that August evening. It was cold and I put the towel I had brought over you, the way you cover something shameful, and you said *You did it because it's over, isn't it, what we had . . . ?*, and your skin was all wet. *You don't want to catch a cold*, I whispered, and you planted a kiss on my lips, put your fingers to your lips and pensively said *It's over . . . it really is over.* Your lips were bluish white, and I just squeezed your hand as you said *I hate you, Camille, I hate you—do you get it?* Your words felt like cigarette burns on my skin; I thought it would crack like clay; then you stood up and said *See you back at the house. Leave me alone.* You dived head-first into the lake and I went home. In the bathroom, I scrubbed my dirty feet red.

I press the back of my hand to the teacup and the red liquid sloshes up to the rim; I remember your sweaty fingers that August evening, and Rudolf saying *But we're friends, aren't we? Friends do things like this for each other,* and while Johannes was doing the other I traced the veins along your wrist; like rivers they were, coursing toward a red sea in which your screams vanished, as did your spit on Johannes's face. I was never able to wash away the expression in your eyes, no matter how much soap I used, and your screams grow louder, distort, clatter, and I jump in my skin when you say *I'll clear it up. I'll get rid of it straight away, sorry, it slipped out of my hand*, and the clattering echoes in my ears, the bathroom door creaks, the cold air creeps under my skin, and Michael sits on the lid of the toilet seat and looks at me for a long time, until I say *Watch out, don't walk on the broken china, you two*, and Michael kisses my forehead and says *Let's leave Camille alone for a bit.*

That night he hugs me to his warm chest and says *You loved her, Camille*, and I stare into the darkness, say *I didn't realise I had handed my cup to Smilla; I wasn't aware of it at all.* And

Michael smells of yellow plums, like you. Maybe that's why I liked him straight away, because of the yellow plums and his river-blue eyes, and because he doesn't ask, because he understands me, and because understanding always chirps louder than silence.

I gave you a sliver of moon and locked it in a glass of water, because the water could not wash away the birthmark, only distort it; and because it would not have been fair to keep the whole moon.

dust motes in the air

When the alarm goes off at 6:00 A.M., I reset it for ten; for Lina, so she'll get up and make herself something to eat. Today is Friday; Lina forgot to put the bread back in its wrapper and it has gone hard overnight. Three cigarette butts float in a lipstick-rimmed cup in the sink and the milk in the fridge has a best-before date of 23 February. It's the middle of March. I fill the bottle with water from the tap. Greeny-blue blobs of mould float to the top; the bubbles from the washing-up liquid burst slowly.

On my way downstairs I meet Frau Unterzimmer. She raises her right eyebrow and asks where Lina is.

She's still asleep.

But you've got a sandwich for school, right, she says, cocking her head. Frau Unterzimmer does not like Lina, which is why she thinks I need looking after from time to time. We watch movies then or read a book. Lina has no TV and she can't read either. Frau Unterzimmer's living room is brown and gold. I always sit on the black leather sofa; it squeaks when I move if my skin is very dry, and Frau Unterzimmer sits in her rocking chair, a tartan blanket on her knees. She always sits very straight; she says that's because she used to do ballet. *Oliver Twist* is my favourite movie.

I don't need anything.

But of course you need a sandwich — you want to grow up big and strong, surely.

I pull my jacket down; it's a little bit too short. Last year it still fit me. Lina says I'll be very tall one day but she won't tell me how tall my father was, or whether I look a little bit like him. She says she doesn't even know who he was any more. I gave up asking, but I like to imagine they were happy once, and that in the evenings happiness found its way to Papa the way a cool breeze creeps through the open balcony door; while Lina, if she was cleaning offices at night back then, would come home in the early morning, make herself a cup of coffee and drink it barefoot on the balcony.

I put the straw into the bottle Frau Unterzimmer filled with milk that has a best-before date of 13 April. It's one of those cheap straws, long and thin. Frau Unterzimmer's sandwiches taste of old lady and strawberry chewing gum. That's because of those scented candles she has on her bathroom windowsill. Being happy with Frau Unterzimmer is like playing Memory even if you have a useless memory; like watching *Oliver Twist* so many times that you can speak the characters' lines with them, and still watch it again.

There's a new girl in our class; she has pink trousers. The others say she's so fat she can't fit through the door and that she stinks.

That evening Lina and I play horse racing: I ride on her back from the living-room sofa to the bed in her room; I go *Whoa* to make her stop, I stroke her cheek and kiss her forehead, I whisper *There's a good horsey, good girl, Lina.* Later, Lina says she got milk and she's sorry. *That's okay*, I say, *Frau Unterzimmer gave me something as well.* Lina beats the dust out of the curtains; her coffee goes cold. She smokes too much, and when she starts saying something, the first word is smothered by her coughing. A red flush spreads from the lower half of her right cheek to the bridge of her nose. She presses the back of her hand to it.

I'm a terrible mother, Nils, I know that.

You're a brilliant mother, Lina.

She often says she's a terrible mother. Once I said, *No, that's not true, Mama*, but she frowned and said, *Don't call me that, please, don't call me that.* So I don't call her that any more. Lina is not a mama; Lina is Lina, and a cleaning woman at night, and sometimes a singer — when she's happy and sings old songs that she waltzes to. She has a beautiful dark voice and an even more beautiful face; Lina would make the most beautiful singer of all; she'd wear a red dress and sing into a microphone and the notes would fill the entire room. The dress would have to be backless and her hair would have to be up. Then you'd see the sharp outline of her shoulder blades, the ridge of her spine. Her neck is the most beautiful thing about her, long and slender. She would look like a queen.

I have decided to be friends with Mathilde. I join her during the break, sitting on top of the bench near the big chestnut tree. I don't know what to say but it needs to be something nice. *I like your hair. It's pretty.* She looks me straight in the eyes — hers are blue, and a little bit green, with yellow flecks in between. *They don't like you either*, she says.

Being happy with Mathilde is like chocolate and skipping school. Her laugh sounds best of all when we are on our own in a corner of the yard at break; then it sounds like a beating drum or a bass guitar. Deep tones. Mathilde is music.

A Friday comes along on which Lina has bought Nutella but there's no bread left, and on which she strokes my head and gets up at the same time as me. She laughs a lot and says she's going to the theatre tonight, that a young man has asked her out. She even paints her lips red. I peer through the keyhole and see her swearing in front of the bathroom mirror because the lipstick has broken; she's putting it on with her finger instead.

Sometimes I think that Lina's happiness is naked, like peeled courgettes, naked and raw. Above all raw. Lina doesn't cook her happiness, because she can't cook, and she has no money for spices either.

I invite Mathilde to my house one evening. She brings a packet of chocolate biscuits; we stand in the doorway, leaning against the frame, and she smiles shyly. I feel like sending her home again because Mathilde is not music today, just silence. I ask her if she's thirsty, tell her we've got milk, or apple juice if she'd prefer. She twirls her hair around her fingers and says *No, just water, please*. Out of the corner of my eye I watch her sizing up our kitchen, which is also the living room. We go and sit on the balcony. At some point Mathilde puts her hand on my arm; I jump and drop my glass of water.

Oh, I'm sorry.

Don't worry. I push the broken glass to one side with my shoes.

Do you think I'm pretty? she asks. I shrug my shoulders. Mathilde is not pretty. I smile; Mathilde picks it up the wrong way and kisses my cheek. *I like you, Nils.*

Mhm, I mumble and, later, around nine, I say she really ought to go home, Lina might be back soon.

I am quite sure Lina will not be home before one. Mathilde smoothes her skirt with her hands; her right eye twitches.

Thanks for the water, she says at the door.

Sure.

Okay then.

Her skirt is a little too tight around the middle; her skin bulges over the waistband.

Nils, she goes, putting her hand on my cheek. She is standing very close; her breath smells of milk chocolate. She plants her lips briefly on my mouth; they feel rubbery.

See you Monday. She smiles. The keys on the ring attached to her bag jingle in the stairwell.

I make myself a cup of hot milk and honey and sit on the balcony until the night cools down. Then I go inside. At four I look at the clock for the last time; eventually I fall asleep.

I wake up to the sound of Lina's footsteps on the wooden floor. I call her name; she sticks her head around the door, shapes a kiss and blows it to me. *Go back to sleep*, she says, and when I ask what time it is, she says, *six*. She lies down beside me; she smells of smoke and drink and aftershave.

Being happy with Lina feels like the way I imagine Australia — as if there's nothing but light. Bright light, with dust motes in the air and in your eyes, but mostly you can look right through them.

I kissed a girl today, I say. Lina puts her arms around me and musses my hair.

Does it always feel rubbery?

She laughs.

c.'s smile

When C. introduced herself, she puckered her lips in such a way that an energy tablet or my thumb might have fit between them and said *Hi, I'm C.*

C for what? I ask.

Nothing. Just C, full stop.

I know C. from the three nights we met at the disco, and I know her better than most. At least that's what C. says, or shouts rather, because it's so noisy at the bar. I say, *In the last three hours you've said No Way too often — I know that much about you.* C. leans over to me, her breath on my cheek, her voice in my ear. *And you never look at people when you're talking to them — did you know that? Your eyes always look past them.* C. tips my nose with her index finger. I don't know what she wants to hear, so I look away and say *Sorry, what did you say? I can't hear you. Too loud in here.* And she smiles her gap-toothed smile, waves a dismissive hand.

Later, C. hands me her glass while she fixes her T-shirt, tugging at the hem; the red drink burns and scratches in my throat; I cough, she thumps me on the back. Do I want to dance, C. asks. I shrug my shoulders. She giggles, *Me neither*, and drags me by the hand out of the disco, saying *Come on, let's go to my place.*

Sitting on the railway bench, C. takes her shoes off; her heels and big toes are red and chafed. She massages them with her fingers.

What do you think would happen if there was no such thing as time? She leans back and strums the air in front of her abdomen like an imaginary guitar, says you have to put your ear to the belly of the guitar to hear the notes vibrate. She tucks her hair behind her ear, leans forward and asks again:

What would happen, do you think? She pretends to put the guitar down on the ground beside her and lifts a finger to her lips, which could mean *Don't stand on it* or *Don't tell anyone*, though who knows what I'd have had to tell, except perhaps that *C. likes playing air guitar.* Before I've said more than *Ehhm,* C. cuts me off with a hand and fishes her phone out of her pocket; it's vibrating. She answers, says *Yes*, then a few more Yeses followed by question marks and exclamation marks. Especially exclamation marks.

Our train comes up on the passenger information display. Platform 3, and we're on Platform 4. *Come on*, I say. C. turns her head away, saying *Yes* into the phone, this time with an exclamation mark and a snort at the end. I look for somewhere I can safely touch C. and tap her on the shoulder in the end, and she tosses me a *Yeahyeah*.

C. shoves the phone back in her pocket and looks at me; her face is illuminated by the station lights. When C. blinks, her contact lenses shift, then slide back into position.

Well, what would happen?

I shake my head, they're announcing our train — *Attention please, Platform 3, the regional train is now arriving, please stand back.* — *Shit*, I say, and C. suddenly grabs my hand, jumps down onto the tracks, I say *No* and she says *Yes,* and I'm running already, C.'s laughter behind me. *Scaredy-cat,* she calls out, and I want to shout *Run faster!* I don't hear her running, only laughing. I see the headlights of the train; they burn blue spots into my retinas. I run, no, stumble more like, across the tracks, the light glaring into the corners of my eyes — *Don't turn round* — haul myself up onto the platform. *I don't usually do this kind of thing, C., this is stupid, plain stupid*, I say, expecting a *So what?* and C.'s laugh to follow — but I hear neither.

Only the screech of train brakes, then voices weaving in and out and over and under each other; someone pulling my arm, pulling me away from the platform, saying *Don't turn round, don't turn round*, whispering *All that . . . You need a wash, a change of clothes — no, don't turn round — come with me.*

Someone puts a hand on my back, then the hand strokes my cheek; it smells of blood; everything smells of blood and — *Don't turn round!*

They told me when C.'s funeral is happening and what her favourite flowers are: callas lilies. They told me she has a first name and a surname, that her name is Cristina Steinberg. I shrugged my shoulders and thought of her eyes reddened by her lenses, her laughing *Scaredy-cat*, and I thought about her being so close that she was already far, far away. I cannot imagine C. dead. Death is a chess board, a series of black and white squares. Death and C. do not go together. I am ashamed of my thoughts. *That's the shock*, they say.

What do you think would happen if there was no such thing as time?

If C.'s phone hadn't rung, I would have said *Haven't a clue.*

It might be . . . good? Now I think I probably wouldn't know what to do, would just stand there and count my breaths until time was restored.

Inhale. Exhale. Nothing else. Full stop.

i don't know

I can't play another note. I've had it up to here. Paula only ad-mitted this once and that was shortly before she threw up on the piano. It was a Friday; by Sunday the piano was in the basement, and two weeks later it was in a house belong-ing to a family who might have been called Müller or Mayer or Goldschmied. I'd like to have known if Paula's piano was in the Müllermayergoldschmieds' kitchen, as it had been in our house; I'd like to have sent them a letter saying: *Pianos belong in the kitchen.*

You can't do that kind of thing, Paula said, but what she meant was: *We need to talk about the past, when I still made sounds and hadn't stopped*, and her mouth was a straight line, and I said, *I don't give a shit.*

Paula has small fingers; she can fit all five into a standard wine glass.

Time trickled in Paula days and Paula nights back when Mother knew our names, minor chords produced by her lungs. Nights with Paula burned in the sound field that rolled up in her ear. Next morning the black had to be scraped off the bodies: Paula's cheek, her forehead, the corner of her mouth and her tongue plummeted to the grass like a shot-down bird.

Paula, I say. Then my words break; I can't quite place the cracking sound—a bit like shells, a bit like bones maybe. *Paula*, I say, addressing Paula's back, because on nights like these Paula no longer has a face, just a back and two hands.

Paula, I say, but she doesn't turn round; her spine straightens and lengthens when she plays the piano; she looks like she's being watched by a cat, and I want to say *Paula,* want to touch her, want to hold her, want to want to want to —

I wake up. *It was only a nightmare,* says Paula, *I'm here. I'm not leaving, I'm here,* and her kiss on my cheek does not belong there.

Whenever Mother shouted *Come on! Who's going to help me hang up the washing?* she always meant me, and it was always me who sported the blotchy red handprint on my cheek later. It was never Paula, and that was what mattered before, only that. Through the kitchen window, from the garden, I tried to see Paula's outline at the piano, and sometimes the light fell just right. When Paula played the piano, her face was a derailed train.

I remember, says Paula. Her right eye is twitching. *I remember her sitting at the kitchen table once — she was always sitting at the kitchen table, oncetwicethreetimes — and at some point she started cutting up banknotes, with a blue rusty scissors —* Now I have more, look how much more money I have, *she said. Do you remember that?* Paula would never have said anything like that before, but then Paula never said anything before, for Paula was a piano then, and at school she was called Thepianoplayer, not Paula. That's all they said, Thepianoplayer, nothing else, except to ask why she always locked herself in the music room during breaks, whether she ever ate anything, whether she could only read music or books as well, whether she could only look serious or could laugh as well, whether she could only play music or could dance as well. People asked a lot of questions. Mostly they asked me. And I knew next to nothing about Paula, only about her back and her hands. *I don't know.* That's my line; I never learned any other. *I don't know.*

These days I like to get Paula drunk, to hear her snore. For Paula could not possibly be any less of a sound. I like the rings under Paula's eyes when she goes to bed too late, her uncombed hair, and when she spatters tomato sauce on her white blouse. Then I dip my finger in the tomato sauce too and wipe a stripe on my collar, put my arm around her shoulder and say, *We're twins, Paula, you and I.*

I learned that Paula is a piano and not a Paula, and even since we sold the piano, if I wake in the morning and her room is empty, I still often think Paula must be sitting at the piano, reduced again to the back of her head and the nape of her neck. But she comes back from the shops or a walk and laughs at me when I tell her *You were rectangular and black again.*

Paula. Paula. Paula. I never heard her name from anyone else's mouth the way it sounded from my mother's. Paula-paulapaula, that was Mother's word, that and: piano.

At concerts, Mother folded her arms under her breasts, said *Paula* and *Piano* and smiled and was proud.

Ina. That was a word Mother did not know. And while Paula and Piano were also among the words she had forgotten in the end, not knowing something and forgetting something are not the same thing.

Paula looks her loveliest when she stumbles into the kitchen in the morning in her nightdress and cradles her coffee cup in her hands; when she drinks the coffee too fast and stubs out her cigarette in the dregs. Then I am the bit of tobacco stuck to the bottom of the cup.

I threw clay onto Mother's coffin and I can't forget how she used to comb my hair, says Paula.

The windows need cleaning — look, I say.

We should be quiet more often, I say, but she should be quiet more often is what I mean. My eyes are trapped in the pattern on the tablecloth; it is hard to look Paula in the eye. It was just as hard to look Mother in the eye while her fingers fumbled with the bottle and she said *I made the elderflower cordial myself.* How I remember that look, morning, noon and night, Mother's look; how it collapsed back into her, over and over at every word, how it questioned and searched and groped, and I said *Yes, it's very nice, you did a great job.* I ventured a smile when she said things like that, but it snagged halfway through the barbed air. At some point, Mother's Yes became very faint, her What and How and Where lying like cigarette butts and sweet wrappers at the kerbside, her Ina forgotten, and only her Paula still as wide as the sky outside in spring.

I wanted to lie on the piano and hear what notes I would strike, and while I wanted to but couldn't — because the piano belonged to Paula, was Paula, not me — the door creaked, then the floor, and father said softly: *The hospital rang*, and I blinked four, maybe five times, stills of him propped in the doorway. Paula screamed; she had wanted to have Mother back here before — before . . . well, for a while, two or three days maybe. Her face was loud, her screams too. A few nodding heads, some swallowing, sobbing, a furry tongue. A lot of gravel-path steps to the grave, dried-up flowers, wet fingers and faces, and *Mothermothermother.* And always the shell's roar in my ear and under my skin, and us pounding the shell with knives until it broke — no ocean in there, no roaring after all. A day later, I saw the girl with the straight-line mouth cry for the first time, and suddenly I had a sister.

Paula was silent in the morning, at noon, at night. People never asked were we twins, just *But you're so different.* I liked that, because their question was a statement, and the statement was *Paula is odd.*

Paula was something that did not belong here, and since Paula and I were so different, that meant I was something that did belong here, and because I belonged here, I was something people understood, whereas with Paula they could never find the right buttons to press. Paula painted all the keys on her piano black.

Paula is odd is the only sentence people say.

I don't know is mine.

The rest is silence, Paula, the piano.

What I longed for back then, after Mother died, was someone who wept with their hands. Someone like Paula. I told her this much later and asked, *Why did you give up? My hands are too small,* she said, and I said, *That's no reason,* and she said, *Just shut it, Ina.*

After Mother died, Paula never played another note, clammed up, and Father had no idea what to do with a piano that had its mouth sewn up and two girls who sat naked on the piano stool drinking red wine at midnight, or with the wrong daughter, who pressed the keys down so slowly that they only made a gentle clunk. But Father had even less of a clue what to do with the right daughter, who suddenly no longer had notes under her skin or in front of her mouth but only words on her skin and in her mouth.

I love her, says Paula; *She loves me*, says Paula, when she's talking about Mother. She never says *I loved her*, and she certainly never says *She loved you* or *She loves you*. All she says is *I can still remember*, trying to weave a fishing net out of every vowel, and weeping with her voice and her words until I bite through her net, because I don't feel like playing fishing, least of all a game of Kill-Ina-and-Skin-Her. Paula likes playing that game, and usually she wins.

Paula and I, slouched on the sofa. Sixth anniversary. Paula has been crying a bit. I'm sliding the catch on her necklace round to the back of her neck when Paula suddenly grabs my hair and says, *Maybe she wouldn't have liked me this way; she wouldn't, she would have —*

Rubbish, I say, but Paula's right. She has been talking too much about dying and death and Mother, and it sounds all wrong — it only sounded right in the notes Paula used to play before.

YesYesYes, Paula says. *She would hate me*, she says, and she covers my mouth with her hands, going *Shh shh shh*.

Paula has small fingers; she can fit all five into a standard wine glass.

Sometimes I can still hear the shells and bones breaking; then I say *Paula*. And if someone were to ask me Whatis-yourname, my answer would be: *I don't know.*

someplace else

She said she knew how it would end. She said, *Let's just run away*. After that she said nothing. Now all I have is the image of her eyes: a close-up, eyelids shut, lashes stuck together with mascara, a hint of smudged aquamarine on the lash line. I try to imagine her blinking; I can't remember the colour of her eyes or the way she looks at me when she smiles or shouts. She said she knew when it would end. She said, *Let's just run away. We can be, someplace else*. Then she measured my silence and hit me over the fingers with the ruler. She knew when it would end. At thirty-nine. I didn't ask what came after that.

The first image I have of Malika is of her calves. The classroom was hot and sticky. It was as if the air had forced itself through the open window, and now it was pressing like a block against my skin. I shoved the hair out of my face, groaning; we were taking a test, I didn't know the answers. There was a knock; I shot a look up at the teacher, who sighed and went to open the door. *Linda, over this way a bit*, my voice a low hiss. Linda slid her answer sheet over. Then there was a girl at the door and the teacher saying *Hand up your answers, folks!* and Linda apologetically pulling her page back again.

I — am — Malika. Her eyes were glued to her shoes, which were nervously tapping the floor. For three weeks I never heard Malika say anything other than *I am Malika*, and *Yes* and *No*. No one ever paid her a compliment, or she might have said *Thank you* as well.

At first I couldn't tell how much Malika understood when little groups gossiped at break time and threw the odd look her way; of course, our teacher had said *Be nice to Malika, make her feel included*, because that's the kind of thing form teachers have to say, but no one thought there was anything interesting about Malika, so the sideways glances were as far as it went.

Later, one time in the dark while I was smelling Malika's fingers, cardamom and sesame, I asked her if those few words really were all the German she knew then. She smiled into her answer. *Do you ask because that was the why for you?* I shrugged my shoulders, my stomach rumbled, and she took me by the hand into her parents' spice shop, made me sit down on the stool behind the counter, disappeared through the bead curtain into the back room, reappeared with three little tins, and I had to try the contents of each. *What do you smell? What do you taste?* I pretended to think about it. She had soon figured out that I couldn't tell cardamom from ginger; and that chilli for me wasn't chilli, just something hot. For Malika, though, every spice had its own meaning, its own healing properties, and that was the *why* for the others; they called Malika a witch because they couldn't think of any other word for the confusion Malika caused.

Malika was neither particularly pretty nor particularly intelligent, and those were the only attributes anyone cared about. Her shoulders were too broad; if a teacher asked her a question she searched for words like someone searching for a needle in a haystack; and her skin smelled neither of perfume nor of cigarettes but of cardamom and sesame. At weekends she helped her parents in the shop and minded the younger ones in the family. That's all I knew about Malika back then and that's all the others ever knew about Malika, and the only other thing they wanted to know was whether Malika was quick to cry and what that crying might sound like.

That's one of the clearest images I have left of Malika: her face when she cries, not a pretty sight. Malika did not react to insults at all, not even when the others shouted *Will your spices punish us now?* and slapped their hands in mockery. At one point I wondered if things might have been different if Malika hadn't made that presentation at school about the spice shop and how they never used prescription medicines at home, only herbal remedies. Later I decided it wouldn't have made any difference; Malika might not have been a witch then, but she'd have been something else.

It was in the darkness of Malika's room that we kissed for the first time too. A little offside first, just above the right-hand corner of her mouth, where two moles lie close together, and only then on the mouth.

In fact, she told me later, it had all happened a bit too quickly for her. I had been in the little spice shop every day for two weeks; the little brown paper bags were piling up in a box under my bed; the sound of rustling chillis had become as familiar as the dripping tap at school. I asked myself what bit of it was meant to have happened too quickly.

Soon after that she had said *We can meet in secret.* I think she didn't want me to get hassled by my friends, and I didn't care what she did or didn't want; with the two of us it was really only about what I wanted, and I wanted Malika. And I wanted the others too. So it stayed a secret, even when we had our graduation party and I danced with Linda all night, because everyone thought there was something going on between Linda and me; even when Linda kissed me on the dance floor; and even when there really was something going on between Linda and me, just enough to stop people forever asking how come I had no time and who was I meeting anyway.

Do you kiss her the way you kiss me? asked Malika, and Linda said *You smell the way Malika smells.* I told Malika that you kiss each person differently and kissed her on the forehead; I pulled Linda into the bathroom, pulled off her clothes and pulled her into the bath.

Basically, things could have carried on like that: I met Linda and the others in the evenings and Malika afterwards, usually at my place, because I didn't want to be kissing her with her younger brothers and sisters screaming in the next room or playing with their Barbies. In the early days I was expecting Malika to end it, what with jealousy and everything, but perhaps it was just that I would have liked to matter that much to her. Looking back, I think Malika did not love me, but she needed someone who loved her, or at least pretended to.

No, it was Linda who ended it all. She drew not one but two lines under it, one under the *we* of her and me and one under the *we* of Malika and me, when she called by my place unannounced one Monday.

Malika and I were lying in the dark, she on the wall side; we had been lying there for so long that I could barely tell where she was, or I, or whether she was at all. Before that, or after or in between, Malika asked me about girlfriends, the ones I had before; I shrugged my shoulders, said that didn't really matter in terms of her and me, and something in her face twisted, just for a second, then she gave a little smile.

I had lit a cigarette and Malika's face had gone a little hazy, when the door flew open.

At first Linda looked from my nakedness to Malika, back and forth and back and forth, then her eyes looked up, into mine. I would have expected her to start screaming instantly, but first she said *Oh*, then the door slammed, Malika's hand sought mine, the door flew open again, and only then did Linda scream, land me a wallop, then another, shove Malika away, forget to close the doors behind her. The silence that followed lay down between Malika and me.

In school the next day Linda started crying; the others looked at me half angrily, half amused. There was a bit of shouting too. And Malika sat in her seat, stared out the window and said nothing. The others thought I had wanted to humiliate Malika, and I didn't stop them thinking that. Things went downhill between Malika and the others in the last few weeks before the summer holidays, and then during the holidays there was a clearance notice outside the spice shop. I have erased the months after that from my memory—all I know is that I heard nothing more of her.

She said she knew how it would end. She said, *Let's just run away*. Then she said nothing. That was on the Monday. We said nothing for so long that I couldn't tell where my body ended and hers began.

She said she knew how it would end, when it would end.

I have a few images of her, nothing else, just the memory of her smell:

Cardamom and sesame.

auntie anna and selma and selma and

Auntie Anna

I say: *Auntie Anna is an artist.* I say: *Auntie Anna has a cat. The cat is called Selma.*

I say this because it is all Auntie Anna can remember now.

I think: Auntie Anna was an artist. I think: Auntie Anna has had sixteen cats. She took the first one and drew it on paper. She drew all fifteen subsequent cats in the belly of the first one. The picture is called *Selma.*

I think this but I do not say it. The sentences lie in my mouth; I wind them around my tongue and bruise them against my jawbones; my jaws grind and the crunching travels to my temples. The sentences going through my head are memories that look forgotten, misplaced, in Auntie Anna's head. They are many film clips, all called: Selma.

Selma 9

When Auntie Anna unhooks the metal door chain, peering through the crack, and says *Ina?*, it's as if she had written the word on a scrap of paper and folded and unfolded it so often that it frays.

Yes, Ina. My breath is big and wide and flows sluggishly out of my mouth. *Hello, Auntie Anna.*

Holding the door wide and laughing, red blotches flaring on her neck, Auntie Anna looks as if she got washed at too high a temperature and shrank; her nightdress and cardigan are at least two sizes too big. I am the only visitor

Auntie Anna has these days, apart from the caregiver, who has no first name, only a surname: Frau Huber.

Nice, says Auntie Anna, *Come in*. Selma 9 winds figures of eight around her ankles.

Film clip 1. Selma 1

I'm sitting on the toilet seat in Auntie Anna's bathroom, brushing my teeth, with Selma 1 curled on my lap; Auntie Anna is cutting my toenails, with her own toothbrush clamped betweeen her teeth. Earlier on I had rung Auntie Anna's doorbell and announced *I'm staying with you tonight*, and Auntie Anna—a paintbrush between the finger and thumb of her right hand, Selma 1 at her right foot—had wiped the green, blue and red studio paint off her face and said *Come on in, then. I've got plenty of cocoa.*

Someone really ought to collect all those toenail clippings; you could make a picture out of them, says Auntie Anna between her teeth, and I ask, *Auntie Anna, why don't you have any children?* Auntie Anna laughs and the toothbrush falls out of her mouth, leaving a broad white stripe on her chin. Back then, all the women I knew were mothers. Except Auntie Anna.

But I have Selma; I have my Selma, don't I? Selma is my baby, says Auntie Anna, and wipes the toothpaste off my chin.

Selma. At that time, Selma was a tabby with brown eyes. That was Selma 1.

Selma 9

Would you like tea, would you like coffee. Auntie Anna doesn't ask, she says and does, as in puts water on to boil. The kettle whistles, she pours the water into the cups, which all have broken handles. *Nice to see you*, she says, smiling; her teeth are yellow and one incisor is missing. Selma curls around Auntie Anna's feet. Auntie Anna microwaves some Alaskan fish for her, laughing at Selma's miaow, saying *All right, all right, just a second, sweetie.* There's paint from the studio on her cheek; I stroke the cheek. It's one of the days on which the paint is fresh.

What comes next is always the same on days when she knows my name. The questions are the same every week; the answers are different every week.

How's school? Auntie Anna asks, and I say, *I'm finished with school, Auntie Anna, I did my Abitur, the week before last, remember? I told you about it.*

Right, right, so you did. But she hesitates too long, her voice breaking on the first *Right* and dragging on the second, so that it really says the opposite. *You're going to New York, aren't you? Like me, right?*

Yes, like you. I breathe loudly, I wait. When Auntie Anna doesn't say anything, I say, *My flight is next week. The flight to New York. I'm going as an au pair, for a year.* I put a hand on Antie Anna's shoulder; Selma 9 purrs and rubs her little head agaisnt my feet. *I'll be gone then, Auntie Anna, like I told you, you know, I'll be gone soon.*

Gone. Auntie Anna shapes the word with her lips, breaks her voice on it. Gone. She says the word as if she were saying *Selma*.

Mama will look after you while I'm gone, Frau Huber too. That's what we agreed, you and me, two months ago. I've gone over this many times; on good days, Auntie Anna just nods, like today, nods and says *I'll be okay.* On bad days she says *Gonegone, like Joachim and me*, and tells me about Joachim and herself, how she went off to New York with him at eighteen because he wanted to open a tattoo studio over there. She tells me how nothing came of the tattoo studio because Joachim could not stick a needle into skin without fainting.

What she doesn't say is that nothing became of her either, except for the sentence *I paint*; and that more should become of me than did of her or that sentence.

Film clip 2. Selma 3

It's the most beautiful memory I have of Auntie Anna. Her lips are red — in her youth Auntie Anna had many lovers; she was very pretty. We are in her studio, which is actually just her basement with pictures on the walls. Earlier, I had asked *May I see your pictures?* The stairs had sighed under our steps; the lock had clicked and the door groaned, then swished open, like wedding dresses brushing parquet floors. *See, there. That one's from Venice.* She's pointing at a painting, but I can't remember it now, or any of them. All I remember is Auntie Anna's eyes, glued to the pictures, and a single sentence: *You remind me a bit of myself, Ina, you know, not just because of the red hair.*

Before, everyone was allowed to see Auntie Anna's pictures. Now she keeps them hidden under white sheets in the basement. *Will you show me your paintings?* I asked Auntie Anna one time since her memory became a hole. She didn't say *No*, she repeated *Will you show me your paintings?*, and settled Selma on her lap, sang her a lullaby.

I was in the basement once all the same, the time Auntie Anna fell on the stairs, when her foot caught on the last step. It wasn't right for me to stay behind in her studio when the ambulance drove off with its siren wailing; it wasn't right to pull back the white sheets and look at the paintings.

But I still remember: the cats' eyes in the paintings were sad, and only one single painting had a motif other than a cat. It was in the right-hand corner of the room: a wrinkly, liver-spotted hand holding two kittens, one with its mouth around the little finger; the other with its front paws hugging the thumb.

Selma 9

What do you want to do when you're grown up, Ina?

Auntie Anna asks the questions and I answer and Selma snoozes on Auntie Anna's lap.

You could paint, I'm sure of it; you paint better than I do. You could be a painter, Ina; you paint better than I do.

I nod, say *'Scuse me,* get up, head for the loo. The carpet underfoot has new stains; I tip-toe to the bathroom door and push it open, my eyes going first: there's hair on the floor, red hair, hair stuck to the mirror, Auntie Anna's hair, lots of it, big clumps. And scissors in the washbasin. *Auntie Anna,* I shout, running along the corridor to the kitchen, through the kitchen to the living room: Auntie Anna is sitting there just as she was, looking out the window, Selma 9 on her lap, her hand stroking its fur backwards, then forwards, backwardsforwardsbackwards. I undo her plait and loosen her hair.

Did you cut your hair yourself? My voice has been sharpened like a pencil. Auntie Annna looks right through me, shrugs her shoulders.

No, no, maybe I was at the hairdresser's.

You did cut your hair, Auntie Anna, I saw it in the bathroom.

She shrugs her shoulders, *I didn't cut it myself,* and I lift Selma off her lap, take her by the hand to the bathroom, to the washbasin, point at the hair everywhere, point at her head. *You did cut your hair yourself.*

Auntie Anna says nothing for ages, and then: *Selma.*

I sigh and say, *I'll do it; go on, you go on over to Selma.* And she smiles and her smile doesn't sit properly in her face.

Film clip 3. Selma 5

It's a Saturday evening. I'm at Auntie Anna's because Mother and Father have gone away. It smells of washing powder and paint. We're drinking white wine; I don't like the wine. At midnight, Auntie Anna decides to cook pasta; she can't find the wooden spoon; we search the kitchen, the living room, then find it in her bedroom, on the bedside table. We laugh, Auntie Anna laughs louder.

Later, the pasta is all stuck together, the tomato sauce is too salty, but who cares, Auntie Anna is an artist, not a cook. We eat the pasta with ketchup. *Enough pepper?* asks Auntie Anna, and I shake my head, and Auntie Anna asks *What do you want to do after the Abitur, Ina?*

I don't know, I say, and I twirl the spaghetti round my fork using a spoon to help. Auntie Anna has a bit of ketchup in the corner of her mouth; she tilts her head and crinkles her eyes, *You don't know. Ah well, you're still young. More pepper maybe?* I say, *You asked me that already*, and her voice sounds like *You're not getting any younger, Ina*, and *You must become a more famous painter than I did.*

In the film clip, it was a Saturday night. That was the start of it. I've been thinking about it a lot lately. That must have been the start of it because this is how it went: on the Sunday of the following week, Auntie Anna couldn't remember where she had put her car keys that Saturday; the following week she found her comb in the cutlery drawer; in the following months she forgot about a cake in the oven, and at a family gathering she asked *Can someone give me a lift home later?*, and later, as we stood at the door in the rain and I said *Hey, isn't that your car*, her face was like a train derailed.

That was the start of it. Ever since, forgetting has been erasing what's in Auntie Anna's head, devouring everything. Except Selma.

Selma 9

I scoop the bundles of hair off the dustpan into the bin and put the brush back in the cupboard.

Where was Frau Huber when you were cutting your hair? I ask, knowing that Auntie Anna will have forgotten. I also tell her that I have to go, and she nods and escorts me to the door. She unhooks the metal chain and the threshold is the silence between us, while Selma coils figures of eight around her ankles.

One of her pictures hangs on the wall near the door; she usually points to it when I'm leaving and says, *Who painted that? I don't like it.* But today isn't usually; today she says *You can do better, you're going to be an artist, Ina, a famous painter. And I'm going to go blind, or deaf, one of the two, whichever is worse — or no, something much worse, something that won't be any help when it comes to dying.* Her eyes bore into mine as she speaks. I feel like lying, like saying *Nothing worse, Auntie Anna, nothing worse*, but she asks, *Who will remember me later, Ina?*

It's not often that I'm glad she'll have forgotten what we talked about by the time I visit her again.

Film clip 4. Selma 7

We're standing outside Auntie Anna's bathroom. She has locked Selma in there. It is late afternoon.

Since yesterday, she says, *I just couldn't take it any more. I told her to be quiet, she hissed and spat, so I locked her up.* The tissues she's holding up to her cheek quiver, all wet and crumpled. We'll have to let Selma out, I tell her, but Auntie Anna says *No*, and *No* again, then gets loud, wailing that there's certain things she won't put up with. Selma didn't normally behave like that, she screams and shouts. I take Auntie Anna in my arms and keep stroking her back until she calms down.

When I let Selma out of the bathroom later, she leaps onto my leg, tearing at my jeans, digging her claws into my skin. She hisses and arches her back. The floor is covered in faeces and urine. This is the only evening I've seen Auntie Anna cry. *She's mad at me*, she says, when Selma's sitting at the other end of the sofa and hissing every time Auntie Anna reaches out a hand to her. With tear-stained eyes, Auntie Anna looks the way she must in fact look: old and left behind.

Selma 9

I have to go, Auntie Anna, I say, and Auntie Anna says, *I don't want to be forgotten*, and Selma purrs and chews her slipper. I nod and say, *I won't forget you.*

Don't forget me in New York, she says, fast and in a very soft voice. *I'll phone you.* I'll do that, I will ring and tell her that I did the *Abitur*, that I'm in New York, and that the woman who comes in every day is Frau Huber.

You must become an artist, says Auntie Anna, with a smile. I nod, say nothing. I did tell her once that that's not what I want, that I can't paint. She had forgotten it by the next visit.

Auntie Anna

I say: *Auntie Anna is an artist.* I say: *Auntie Anna has a cat. The cat is called Selma.*

I have four film clips and two visions.

Vision 1: We are in Japan. Auntie Anna is cutting off Selma 9's little ears, then her tongue, then her little legs. She puts the little ears, the tongue and the little legs in the fridge and forgets about them.

Vision 2: We are in Japan. Auntie Anna is frying Selma's belly and head in olive oil in a pan and cutting into the meat with a knife to see if it it's done.

This is my vision of Auntie Anna. I can picture Auntie Anna like this.

before max came

She likes the sound of the wheels rolling over the tarmac as the plane prepares to take off, the crackling as the air presses in on the sides, shimmers over the wings; she likes the rattle of the folded-up tables in the seats in front. She likes the feeling when the air turns to granite, when her stomach is sucked towards her heart and her skin plays cat-and-mouse—she is the cat, her skin the mouse, and her skin ends up inside the cat. White vapour trails in the sky leave images in her ears—the aeroplanes are always inaudible.

Sure, she has seen one photo of Max. She studied it from different angles in the image editing program, until at 80 degrees his smile looked serious. Max and seriousness, that's a good combination, and the upside-down smile looks right too. In the normal view she couldn't get a handle on this Max who looked like he'd say *Please, go ahead, I'm not in any hurry* to an old lady in the supermarket queue, or help a young woman with a child and a buggy onto the train.

Blind date, she thought, and rotated Max by 35 degrees. The words did not look familiar at any angle.

Hey, how's it going, Max had written—no question mark, but she'd read it with one anyway. Ever since, she's been imagining this: how.max.will.say.*hi*.how.he.will.say.*hey. how's.it.going*; how he might put his arm around her, how she might run shy fingers along her collarbone.

Their silence will be the kind of silence you get free of charge from the supermarket check-out girl as she scans a packet of chewing gum; and their smile will be the kind of smile bestowed on the back of your hand by the ticket-takers in the cinema. He.will.say.*hey.how's.it.going.* She bites her lip; all she can see out the window is clouds. The stewardess is holding a tray in her right hand. Orange juice. No. Sparkling wine. Yes.

Her case is the last one bumping along; she lifts it off the belt. *Colmar train station, at the SNCF ticket office near the newsstand.* The button on the train door lights up green; in moments like this she'd like to chop her head off and carry it along at her side: what.will.max's.room.look.like.what.will.it. be.like. Happynewyear, orangejuicenosparklingwineyes.

Fireworks and bubbly, that's New Year's Eve, he said, and that he didn't drink orange juice. She couldn't help thinking about his lips. She cuts the mouths out of the faces of the people walking by, rushing by rather, and stuffs the ones she likes best into her jeans pocket.

Hi, she said, and later *Good morning* and *Sleep well* and *Yes*, always smiling, and her skin was too far away. She found herself again in the morning, in the bathroom, wedged between the shower door and the tiled wall; the hot steam piled up against the glass; she wished it was Max in there having a shower.

It feels colder than minus 3 degrees Centigrade; the cold stings her eyes and she pulls her hat down over her forehead. The streets are sheets of snow crunching under her soles; here, time must be almost glass-like, which isn't a good fit for Max. Max's words are made of birch bark; you can peel them off. That's how she imagines his voice too: wooden.

I might not be what you expect, she had written. *Yes.* It read as if it ended with a full stop. No sign of a comma or a clause like *I might be different too*.

She pushes her hair back and straightens her skirt in the shop window. *You look absolutely gorgeous*, the sales assistant with the rose-tinted voice had said on Tuesday; when she looked in the mirror, she did think she was gorgeous. Now it doesn't feel like Tuesday any more.

Three stops. The doors will open on the left. There isn't much room in the toilet; she takes off her hat; the mirror is all streaky; she mouths sentences in a language whose words pass through her teeth like an egg through an egg-slicer. Austria — that sounds like skies full of orchards, like roosting trees from which bird cherries fall. French — that sounds like a blue sphere in which kingfishers glide, and Colmar sounds like burnt butter.

At the SNCF ticket office, okay, wearing a blue hat, she had written, and he might have laughed. He had replied, *I'll recognise you anyway*, but he was lying — he doesn't recognise her anyway, and she has to dig the hat out of her bag to catch his attention in it. He smiles and says *Iris*, slipping it in between one breath and the next, and it doesn't sound like wood — it sounds like ice-skating without skates.

Hey, how's it going, he says, and *Here we are then*. His accent breaks the words; his vowels are too short; he stumbles on the *then*. She nods. His hands on her back seem heavy; she rests her chin on his shoulder, feels the bones against her skin.

When the air turns to granite and her stomach shifts towards her heart, her skin plays cat-and-mouse with her. And sometimes it's her skin playing the cat, herself the mouse.

Then she is eaten by her skin.

The train arrives and Max helps a woman with a child and a buggy onto the train. He smiles, but she cannot rotate his smile through 180 degrees in her head, nor did he put his arm around her.

pine shoots and fish cans

My granny is a small woman. That sentence is from my school copybook when I was in sixth grade. My granny is a small woman, it says, and: We are exactly the same height.

I used to often say *Granny, tell me about the old days, when you were little* and think of the family trees in the Bible. And Abraham begat Isaac and Isaac begat Jacob and so on, until eventually it was Jesus's turn.

Now I say *Granny, what did you dance to back then*, but Irmi doesn't hear me and rustles the paper, turning two pages in one go. I say *Irmi* and other kids say *Granny* but that word sounds like it's been put on ice. So then I say *Irmi, what did you dance to back then*, and Irmi rustles the paper and folds it, creasing the front-page model's nose in the process and making me think of the Viennese Waltz. I look at her mouth; the smile creeps along her lip lines then tilts backwards inside her.

There's a photo of Irmi and Grandpa in which Irmi is wearing a flared yellow dress. Poised for a waltz, head turned to the camera, Irmi is smiling; she looks like a woman who would perch on the kitchen counter, munching celery stalks, and say to her husband things like *D'you remember how crazy we were back then—d'you remember?*, while her husband stirs the saucepans and asks her to taste little spoonfuls.

When I was young, my father used to say, *there was always too little meat for dinner, and Father always ate every bit of what little there was. We got the leftovers*. And I see a different Irmi to the one in the flared yellow dress with her head flung back, who powdered her nose just before she took to the dance floor: now I imagine her inside a fish can with two air-holes punched in the lid.

When I'm at Irmi's she never puts the radio on. It was like that years ago too, when we used to play Memory and it mattered more to me that I picked the prettiest pairs of cards, not the most.

The Beatles, that's what we used to dance to, says Irmi, and it doesn't suit the waltz. *The Beatles*, says Irmi, and she can't speak English. *The Beatles*, says Irmi, and her real name is Irmgard.

I didn't hear that from Irmi; Father told me one time, when I was eight. I remember thinking it was a secret and observing Irmi for weeks, whenever we played Memory or when she was buttering bread in the kitchen; I held the name Irmgard up beside her head and giggled and bit my tongue so that I wouldn't shout out *Your name is Irmgard. I'm not allowed say who told me, and it's a secret and I know that and I won't tell anybody.*

When I was younger I was here on Tuesdays and Thursdays, and sometimes on Saturdays, and Irmi was my friend. Now I'm here a couple of times every six months, and I could count the number of times over all those months on two hands. And I don't say Irmi now, I say Granny. I only say Irmi now if I'm talking about her, like saying *I'm going to Irmi's*, and when Irmi opens the door and looks small there in the doorway, I say *Hi Granny*.

In the hallway, Irmi is a dropped stitch, a tone so high-pitched the ear no longer perceives it, and when we're sitting at the table and she calls out from the kitchen, *Do you want*

*a drink of water ... oh, did I forget to give you a glass? ...
Would you like raspberry juice? I've got some cordial, and how
are you anyway? Wait ... oh, you've got yourself a glass already,
I'm sorry, I forgot* ... then I could chop Irmi up on the smallest chopping board, the green one for vegetables, and let her
melt in the smallest saucepan. She would fit into my water
glass and she wouldn't say *No* if I wanted to drink her.

Irmi is afraid that everyone knows, about Grandpa and E.
Irmi does not say *No*; she has never said it. For some reason,
Irmi always tends to fall in curves; I have an image of her
having corners at one time, but she filed them off with every
woman who came along who had neither a name nor a face,
until E. came along and had four corners, but by then there
was no more room for the corners; by then Irmi was already
a curve.

Father said *Irmi's not a very strong woman*, and I said *Yes
she is*, and he laughed and shook his head and all of a sudden
I was all hands and nothing else.

The red fingerprints on his right cheek were visible for
a long time.

Granny, what did you dance to back then? I say, and Irmi
doesn't hear me. *Irmi, what did you dance to back then*, I ask,
and her eyes are a *No* and her words turn inwards.

When I hug her, I'm afraid she might fall apart. I'd like
to ask her, *Granny, tell me about the old days, when you were
little*, and *Granny, are you mad at Grandpa, are you jealous
of E.?* but instead I evade her watery gaze when I invite her
to the movies and say *No* when we're standing at the ticket
counter and she fishes the money out of her bag.

After days with Irmi I feel like going back over all the

routes she has taken and picking Irmi up off the streets. I think about the woman in the flared yellow dress, who may have been called Irmgard, and about the Irmi whose lights are always out by nine or ten in the evening and who retraces her steps around the house every day with the vacuum cleaner, hoovering up the little bit of Irmi and putting it in the black refuse sacks that are put out on Wednesdays.

They used to sit side by side in the clubhouse, Irmi and Grandpa, occupying two of the four or six judges' seats. After each round, I would collect the diamanté that fell off the dresses and scattered to the edges of the dance floor. The Latin dancers' short red dresses were my favourites. Sometimes Father would take me in his arms, or later, when I was a bit older, he'd bend down to me; then we'd dance around the perimeter, and if Grandpa was doing the scores, he'd always smile at us and hold his two hands up, fingers splayed. It was Grandpa too who showed me how to waltz, but I only ever saw Irmi dancing once; that was when Grandpa had a new house with four corners, in which no one waltzed any longer, and when I needed a room in which to practise with J., who was like butter and whom I always washed off my skin when I showered in the evenings. And so, because of J., the butter, and me, though I was no bread, Irmi brought old records up to us in the attic; she danced around the room with my father, wearing black leggings and an oversized white sweater, with her head thrown back, and looked just like the woman in the yellow dress.

Irmi, what did you dance to back then? I ask, and her look is like a hook; she rams it into a soft cushion. I could also ask, *Granny, why don't you listen to music any more?* and *Granny, how did Grandpa propose to you and did you get to know him through dancing?* I picture a woman at dancing lessons, smiling as she leans against the wall, then I picture Grandpa asking her to dance just as the music is switching from "The Blue Danube" to "Que Sera, Sera," and how the pianist bungles a note or two and the woman flinches.

For two years now the look in Irmi's eyes has been an apology, a room with the door left open, the last 40 grams of a 160-gram potato when the recipe only requires 120 grams. When people say *There's always something left*, I can't help but think of Irmi, and I've only seen Grandpa twice since two years ago. Both times it was winter; once in early November, the year Grandpa went to Spain with E. for Christmas, when they were still living in S., in a small apartment on the tenth floor. We had pasta with tomato sauce and Auntie waited outside in the car and didn't want to say *Hi*, not to mention *Hi Papa*, and all I can remember is that it made no difference whether you were standing outside on the balcony in minus 2 degrees Centigrade or sitting inside at the table. A second time, Grandpa rang, but he only rang Father, not Auntie, and said *What would you like to eat?* and *Wednesday, will we make it Wednesday?*, and the apartment had given way to a small house with three floors connected by steep spiral stairs, and E. smiled and looked serious at all the right moments. And I remember how I flinched when Grandpa said *So . . . here's the bedroom*, and over the bed there was a photo of E. and Grandpa in which E. was smiling just like the woman in the flared yellow dress. It was minus 5 degrees then, and there was a difference between the temperature on the balcony and at the table, but none between the balcony and the way home, when Mother and Father were discussing how on earth it would work with the spiral stairs and the three storeys and a wheelchair, and I said *Stop it!* and kept thinking of Grandpa's eyes, the way his gaze hovered over our faces, as if looking for somewhere to land, and of his smile, which I had to avoid when I hugged him and said *Bye.*

Irmi, tell me about the old days, I plead, when I'm eleven, and Irmi says that they boiled pine shoots to eat, and they had no shoes and no father, though you could make the former out of sardine cans. That's what Irmi says, and she doesn't cry, and I put my arms around her because otherwise she might fall apart. Irmi has talked to me a lot about the past but she hasn't told me much, and now when I ask her I'm afraid she'll cry, because she won't be telling me about pine shoots and sardine cans and The Beatles but about "The Blue Danube" and "Que Sera, Sera."

When I was younger I was here on Tuesdays and Thursdays, and sometimes on Saturdays, and I say: *Irmi, may I call you Granny?* She says yes.

Now I'm only here a few times every six months, and I say: *Irmi, Granny, may I call you Irmgard?*, and Irmi is not a strong woman and *que sera, sera*, and Irmi hoovers the house in the mornings and is a dropped stitch and the left-over 40 grams of a 160-gram potato. *May I call you Irmgard, IrmiGranny?* I ask, and now you can only see three-quarters of the model's nose on the front page of the paper, and Irmi says: *No.*

nighthawks

I

We're sitting on the heater in Noah's living room. Noah says *You have to start something new before you end something old.* I'm not sure I understand what he means; I'm frequently not sure I understand Noah. *Ha?* I go, and his face looks too round with the short haircut. *You have to be dead before the dying is over,* says Noah. I can only relate Noah's talk of dying, of the new and the old and death, to one Noah-image in my head: Noah killing fish, removing the hooks, whacking them on the head until the tails stop flailing. Noah gutting fish, slitting their pale bellies, spilling out the guts. *I sell fish, on Saturdays at the market,* he said, lining the swim bladders up in front of him. *Watch this, listen — they each make a different sound when you step on them.* Noah can play "Five Little Ducks" on these swim bladders.

III

It was a Thursday when Ben's blue Renault crashed into the tree and Noah's teeth bit into my belly. The call came while Noah was putting the kettle on — Noah didn't look good making tea in the nude, and I liked that. I don't remember the secretary's exact words now, just her voice, her low-fat-margarine voice. *Hospital.* She repeated this word several times, and she may well have said *You must come immediately.* Because Ben needs me now, because I ought to be there for him — those are lines from rose-tinted movies, and while I enjoy watching them, I have no desire to act them out.

Noah didn't ask what was wrong; in fact, he never asks much anyway ... I didn't go to the hospital that evening, nor any other evening that month.

II

Mia, says Ben, feeling his way along the edge of the living-room table towards my footsteps. I stop moving and breathe very quietly. If I keep quiet for a long time, Ben won't be able to find me.

You don't have to stay with me, says Ben, raising the wine glass slowly to his lips; the rim bumps into his nose.

I think about the Ben I fell in love with as he played the piano on stage; he could fill any space when he played, no matter how big. Later I watched him leaning at the bar, his right hand holding a martini, his left round a girl's waist. He bent down to her, his teeth finding her earlobe, his gaze snaring everything in its net.

I wanted to be a piano for Ben.

I

Noah and I are in the kitchen; I'm cutting courgettes into julienne sticks; Noah is halving the onions the wrong way, through the middle, and the layers are falling apart. *The only thing I can cook is fish,* he says, and I look at his hands on the chopping board. Noah has big hands, exactly the right size for my breasts.

When I'm at Noah's, water builds up in my lungs; when I sleep with Noah, I feel too old for him; the way his lips don't quite fit mine when we kiss, the way his whole body trembles when my hand drifts under his waistband. When I sleep with Noah I always leave the light on, to see his ruddy cheeks; his mouth feels its unseeing way up and down my body.

III

I loved undressing Ben after a concert, when the notes were still there under his skin, when his tongue painted rivers on my skin, when he let them dry, then found them again. *I'm a pianist*, Ben said, the first time we met. Dinner in a Chinese restaurant; the sushi didn't agree with me; he held my hair out of my face later, when I had to throw up. I sell bread and rolls—I didn't say it, but it would have been true.

Ben and I, we had mouths and hands only at night, and mostly only at weekends. *Ben is away a lot*, that's what I said to Noah before I kissed him for the first time. That was the best thing with Ben—imagining the other. Imagine, I'd say to myself when Ben wouldn't ring from Monday to Friday, when I'd make lasagne, his favourite dinner, and the sheets of pasta would fall apart in the water; imagine, imagine. I loved the thought of a Ben taking someone else's finger in his mouth.

Now it makes no difference whether we make love in the dark; it makes no difference whether I say: *I'm afraid you won't like what you see*, or *Why Noah? Because Noah doesn't look good in the nude.*

Ben's tongue still roams over my skin but he's no longer able to find the dried-up tributaries.

I

Are you going to stay with him, why are you staying with him? Noah hasn't asked me that, but Ben would have, had things been the other way round. Noah just goes *Hmm* and shows me a photo of a carp gasping for air, the same one that's frying in the pan right now. I feel like saying *je t'aime* or *te queiro* to Noah, and saying it often, because it's not the same as *Iloveyou* and it means I could lie to him, since he wouldn't know the difference. Noah is a bit dim; I like that.

II

MiaMiaMia — Ben says that a lot, as if he's forgotten who I am.

I miss that little tug beneath my skin when one of Ben's girls rang, when he'd say a soft *Hey! How are you* into the phone and leave the room, when he laughed and his voice sounded like smoke and scuffed leather.

You don't have to stay with me, Ben says. He says it only once, on a Thursday two months after *It was a Thursday*. And at midnight he sits at the piano, fingers resting on the keys, pressing them down slowly, just the skeleton notes; his breath comes too fast; he plays the A above middle C three times, then folds his hands in his lap.

You don't have to, I say, *Maybe it's too soon*. He says I should keep my trap shut, and suddenly he's the Ben I fell in love with.

We try to be silent. Ben is better at it than I am. I say: *I know* — but that's a lie and Ben is not the least bit dim. *It wouldn't be fair* — I go red when I say that.

There are only a few wine glasses left in the house; most of the rest are in the bin, in smithereens.

I

I sell fish, on Saturdays at the market, Noah had said, and I'd said *I sell bread rolls.*

I like fish, Noah had said. *I like the yellow bags we have in the shop, with red italic lettering on them*, I'd said. I like the woman who has a latte every morning at nine, over in the right-hand corner by the window. I like topping cappucinos off with milky foam, and the sound of fresh crusty rolls breaking. I never told Ben this; Ben was a pianist, Ben wasn't there during the week and didn't ring me either, and he never wrote a song for me, even though I'd always wanted him to.

I find it hard to say *is* and not *was* when I talk about Ben. It's not fair to say *was*. But I do it anyway.

Ben was a pianist.

And I sell bread rolls.

And Noah sells fish and plays the guitar. Sometimes he plays for me at three in the morning; he often messes up the F chord. I like the sound of his fingers sliding along the strings.

III

Ben always said I was capable of much more, that being a shop assistant was not for a woman like me. Ben thinks I should be a manager, run a tattoo studio, or a five-star hotel. Ben thinks I should have a career that befits a man like him.

Ben never invited me to any of his concerts. We always met back at his apartment later; I didn't stay if he was leaning at the bar with a glass of champagne, his eyes on the lookout for someone else.

II

It only happened once, that one of Ben's girls rang the doorbell. He was sitting at the piano, his arms folded across his chest, his eyes looking right through the wall, right through me, and he said: *I'm not in.* I'll never forget the way Ben looked when he felt ashamed.

What's the story, you and your boyfriend? Ben asks. He would never have asked that before.

Noah is a bit dim, I say and take hold of Ben's hands, which are feeling the air in search of my voice. His fingers seek out my mouth, my nose, my shut eyes. *I am a pianist*, he says and suddenly grips my face, pulling me into a rough kiss, as if he can see me again.

I

He'll leave sooner or later, I say to Noah. We're lying on the sofa, Noah's blowing mini donuts with the hookah smoke, his face is empty and his voice alcohol-soaked.

I don't talk much when I'm drunk, and Noah doesn't talk much when he isn't. When I come here on Mondays, I bring wine, whiskey and vodka with me. Noah sings and plays the wrong chords on the guitar, and we always drink the wine straight from the bottle.

When I think of Noah, all I see is his mouth and his stomach. When I used to think of Ben, I saw his hands and his eyes.

If I am quiet for a long time, Ben can't figure out where I am any more. I tiptoe across the floor and hold my breath. *Mia*, says Ben. I get undressed and am nothing but sounds: the teeth of a zip, the static crackle of tights, the sigh of a nightdress . . .

Mia, says Ben, *look at me when I'm talking to you*.

That wouldn't be fair, I say. Ben never asked why I didn't visit him in hospital.

I

Days with Noah have hungry maws and line up one beside the other, mouth to mouth. I cut their pale bellies open and lie down in there — Noah always sews them up eventually, the gaping belly flaps.

He'll leave sooner or later, I say to Noah. He puts the white wine to his lips; the bottle clunks against his teeth.

Who are you kidding, says Noah, and suddenly he isn't dim any more.

Mondays, Tuesdays, Wednesdays, Thursdays and Fridays were Noah days. Now I only go to his place twice a week at night; the flat is cold, Noah's hands stink of fish. On Saturday mornings I stand at the flower stall opposite Noah's fish stall; I never buy anything; I avoid Noah's gaze and wish he would say: *Take your clothes off when I'm talking to you.* But that's something Ben used to say, something he locked up in a drawer; and now Ben can't find the key.

III

What's the story with your boyfriend? asks Ben, and I say, *You have to start something new before something old ends.* I slit the days' bellies open the way Noah guts fish and I step on their swim bladders. No matter which order I burst them in, Noah always recognises my "Five Little Ducks." *You don't have to stay with me*, says Ben; if I am quiet long enough with Noah, I forget where he ends and I begin.

He'll leave sooner or later, I say, and Noah shakes his head. At night, when Ben's already asleep, I feel like piercing his chest with a fish hook; or I could use a hammer, or a heavy vase maybe — one blow to the head, then it'd be over. Most people die in their sleep as it is.

flickering lights

We turn to the left, to the right, then left, then right, then

Just for a moment, to no longer know where sound and where image where you where I where beginning where end. Where left where right.

We turn to the left

The floorboards in the bedroom are worn; the light is slanted. My hand strays across the bedcovers to yours; you are breathing through your mouth. I feel like unbuttoning you to see what's under your skin. My theory: you're layered, you're an onion. My theory on changing perspective: the layers overlap; you trim the edges every day where they protrude. My theory when this perspective collapses: you are three notes, a chord.

We turn to the right

Now—yes, now I'd put it differently, now that I'm turning this way round, to the right, it all looks quite different; in fact, it doesn't look at all, it just sounds. The bedroom floor creaked and you addressed my heels in whispered phrases that had a blurred use-by date underneath (and I used to think words would keep forever). You can only see it if you upend it, when the light slants in from underneath and breaks up the words. Now I think it was actually you who unbuttoned me, and there was no theory to it, just certainty.

Soundoffingernailsonthebedcovers.

Your voice fast-forwards and rewinds.

We turn to the left

We carry the evening into the night, hold each other's hands, letting them drift under our clothing, letting them drift down further. It is as if we are divided and held together by lines; I lean against the bedstead, my lips trying to grasp my thoughts. *That's where they'll fall down*, you say. *Soon*, you say.

I don't ever want to know what you would mean to me without hands.

We turn to the right

And all I can remember is the darkness and your hands like an electric storm reaching my wrist, leaving my pulse trailing behind. I don't remember our breath faltering—though it must have. Maybe you remember that bit; I must ask you; perhaps you'd post it to me.

We turn to the left

I feel the edges and corners of your skin. At night, I pretend to sleep and you recite monologues and screw light bulbs into your words, but I'm afraid it's lost on me. There's a toothpaste splash on the bathroom mirror; the bedroom door is open — *that's how our relationship should be too*, you say. Your words are back to front, though I thought there was only one side to them.

We turn to the right

All I remember is: there were so many noises. I melt them in a bain-marie with too much water; it bubbles up. Lower lips getting chewed, hands whispering, skin being inhaled, gazes scratching.

Doors banging.

We turn to the left

Your hands are covering my eyes; *That's the way we're meant to be together*, you say. Your nocturnal monologue is in tatters: *Too hemmed in*; it's cold in bed. *Surely we should be able to have a rational conversation*; I try not to swallow, my mouth is too dry. *This can't go on.* I wedge the toes of my right foot under my left calf. *Who is to blame*; you light a fire under your words; I watch your body fade.

We turn to the right

Blame is a musical note kept behind locked doors. I can't find the right bowl for it in in the cupboard, to melt it in the bain-marie. I remember there were many, many notes. Now all I have in my head is one image: you with a cork in your mouth.

We turn to the left

Now you are screwing bulbs into your words by day as well as by night. I buy a string of lights, drape them around your neck and let you circle around the living room until your shoulders feel heavy. Then I remove the weights bit by bit and try to break the light bulbs without you noticing, but you do notice, and you say *It's not enough, this.*

We turn to the right

The bain-marie with the notes in it is bubbling and spluttering; the notes are melting gradually. I lean in close over the pot; the hot steam presses against my cheeks, spluttering and spitting on my skin.

We turn to the left

Your words are bright; I am blinded. You tie your voice around my neck. I can't breathe. Later you hide my blueish face under big scarves. In the stairwell, you stumble and your bunch of keys falls two floors; the sharp sound as it lands is etched on my eardrum.

We turn to the right

I can't remember any more; I no longer know what happened.

We turn to the left

Ginger tea and pizza—that's a dreadful combination, you say. *Maybe that's why I like it*, I say. You're sitting on the big sofa, I'm on the little one. Your skin is too far away and your words are too near. I am a silence. You are a hot-water bottle with a hole in it; you are leaking. *Whose fault is it?* My eyes look past yours; I measure the silence after you say, *Then I'll leave*. Doors bang. At some point I run out of tape to measure the second silence.

We turn to the right

I no longer know what spoke into the silence.

We turn to the left

You shoved your words into the light bulbs and left some behind for me. You see the end, but not what's beyond it.

We turn to the right

Tram atmosphere. Third stop. The overhead light strip hums. The wheels rasp. There's a light on in your place. The living-room window is tilted open; the wind gusts around the house. The tarmac fast-forwards and re-winds.

We turn to the left

I no longer know what it was that reached into the silence.

Do your light bulbs still flicker?

We turn to the right

I leave the bain-marie of melted notes at your door. Inside, I can hear voices. A short while later, the light goes out. I turn to leave.

We turn to the left, then to the right, then left, then right

For just one moment, to no longer know where sound and where image where you where I where—

fatherland

one

Someone who looks at someone else the way you pinch the skin off hot milk.

Someone who puts their fingers in their mouth, inserting into each gap someone with their eyes to the wall. Someone who raises a hand, and not just to brush back their hair.

Someone who undresses someone else the way you chop wood, and someone who touches someone else the way you swat flies.

Someone who dies and someone who doesn't; and what is left behind in people's mouths.

two

Sunday evening. It's very hot. Eiske's head is propped on her hands and she's looking at the son.

Marie, says the son and looks at Eiske.

Yes, says Eiske and looks like Marie.

Marie, says the son and rips Eiske's stomach open, piling the weight of the last few days into it, the mother's face, the father's face, and whatever lies between. Then he closes Eiske's stomach, sewing it up in a hurry—he will need it again next week.

MarieMarieMarie, says the son.

The son loves Marie, Marie does not love the son, and the son loves Eiske—as long as he can pretend she's Marie.

Eiske picks at a scab in the dip of her collarbone; she sees dried blood from a mosquito bite on her fingers. *You are your father's son*, she says and that's something Marie would never say, says the son to himself, and suddenly Eiske is Eiske again, and the son gets up, says nothing, leaves silently. That is one of those moments in which the son mixes the languages of his parents.

three

It's the father who shoots the deer; it's the father who looks through the binoculars and the son who has to stay still and keep quiet, to wait until the father raises the rifle. The son has to wait and listen for the shot. The eyes of the living deer are his mother's eyes, the eyes of the dead ones the father's.

That last bit is a lie. *For now*, says the son. *Soon*, says the son.

And looks at his hands: the father has very big hands, the biggest of all of them. And the son looks on in silence and places a sprig of pine in the deer's mouth while the father dips his sprig in the gunshot wound. *Look*, he says and laughs; his laugh is deep and wide and he tucks the bloodied sprig into his cap, wears the deer's blood on his head.

four

Trees and windows are knives; they cut up the sky.

Smoke escapes from the kitchen window; there's a smell of burnt potatoes. Above the cooker there's a needlepoint picture of a man hunting a deer; the man's legs are stitched in red; that's where the mother ran out of black thread— there and on the hands, in the hands; the hands and legs are dead.

The father sits at the table; his hands and feet are black. The mother twists her neck to see the father. She has a vision of him growing before her eyes, the chair collapsing, the roof becoming his hat and—

The father sweeps the cutlery off the table; it shouts from the floor: *You stand there at the cooker as if you had nothing better to do, nothing except stand there, you stupid woman.* The woman blows at the smoke and pulls the pot off the stove; the potatoes are stuck to the saucepan, their bottoms all blackened. The mother cuts the black bits off and eats them, licking her fingers clean.

That's what I like to see, says the father, laughing. His laugh is thick and sticks to the corners of his mouth. He spits on the floor; the potatoes taste of tears and silence; the father raises his hands, those hands that are so big, way too big, and he hits the mother; his hands are black, are death—but not today.

I'm sorry, says the mother. That's all she says. Every word is a rope knotted around her neck.

five

Sometimes the mother feels like shouting. For example: *Mouths are useless organs; they could all be cut out and tied up in black refuse bags.* Sometimes the mother would like to shout: *Mouthsmouthsmouths are organs that should be thrown out. Who on earth speaks with their mouth these days—does anyone still do that?*

It's like this:

The mother speaks with her eyes.

The father speaks with his hands.

The son speaks his mother tongue less and less fluently.

Sometimes the son feels like shouting. But he doesn't do it. Shouting is the father's language. He doesn't want to speak his father tongue.

The father tongue is very easy. The son speaks it well.

six

It's night time. The father lies on top of the mother, pulling at her blouse, her breasts, her belly, thrusting forcefully into her; the mother is a tree in the desert.

Later: the mother sits at the kitchen table, emptying jug after jug of water; the water keeps trickling from her eyes. The son's steps on the stairs, in the hallway, on the tiles; the son's hands are quick; they hand the mother tissue after tissue, and the mother's mouth opens and closes like a fish, opening and closing and opening and—

The mother stuffs tissues into her mouth, one after another; fifteen cram in. Then she goes out to the garden with her eyes trickling. And in the garden there are violets and roses and trees. The mother waters the plants every day.

seven

The night belongs to the father.

The morning belongs to the mother.

The son belongs to twilight.

eight

In the morning, the bus with the brightly lit windows drives past the house, and the mother knows the son is sitting on the bus in his dusty trousers. The mother is standing at the window; the table is set, waiting for the father. She spreads jam on his bread, she scrubs and she cleans, without looking at the father, until the door shuts behind him. Then she goes outside and opens her mouth really wide. The mother gulps in as much air as she can; she has a cupboard full of empty jam jars which she fills with air for the weekends. *That's better*, the mother says, to no one.

It's like this: At night the father steals the mother's breath. *Woman*, he says, *open your mouth* and the mother yanks her lips apart; her lips scream, not the mother. The father grabs the breath out of the mother's mouth; the father's finger-nails tear the last shreds of the day's breath from her gums. *Woman*, his voice is dark and wide. *Why*. The father doesn't hear the mother; the mother has no voice. *Why*.

nine

Sometimes the mother holds the son up against the midday light. His silhouette is almost an exact match for his father's. When the son comes home at lunchtime, Eiske is waiting for him at the entrance to the apartment block. The rest of the day, Eiske waits at the garden gate for him, in the evenings too. Waits and waits, sitting on the bent gate, picking the windfall apples in the grass; she only picks the rotten ones. Eiske doesn't pick the worms out of the rotten apples; bite by bite the worms find somewhere to die in Eiske's stomach, and while the worms are dying, Eiske eats and Eiske waits. For the son.

Marie does not wait for the son. When the son looks into the neighbour's garden, he sees Marie lying on her tummy in the grass, reading a book; the pages quiver and rustle as they turn. He sees Marie laughing with her friends and painting her fingernails, and her laugh is wide and beautiful, and the nail polish glints in the sun and dazzles him. Marie is beautiful from afar and from the outside. The son has a vision of a beautiful Marie.

The father comes home for lunch and he eats the mother's share.

In the basement, the mother has two deer that the father

shot. Side by side, the two deer lie in the freezer along with other frozen food. On Sundays, the mother hacks a bit off the deer—the legs and a bit of belly are missing already. The knife cuts through the frozen meat as if it were butter. The mother fries the meat in the pan, but only very briefly, so it's still raw in the middle, and only the man gets it for lunch; only the father's plate has deer's blood oozing on it as the knife slices into the meat.

The hours with the father devour the bread out of the mother's mouth, eat the skin off her bones. *You're too skinny; you're ugly; I'll find myself a younger woman*, the father says, tearing the clothes off the mother's limbs and forcing himself into her.

ten

The son has two wishes.

There's this:

The mother glues other people's smiles and voices onto her face. Sometimes things don't sit right; then she takes the scissors; the finger holes make her skin blister. She pulls a smile and a voice over her face, stretching them tight so that no wrinkles form; anything that sticks out over the edge of her face gets cut off.

The son's wish: to pull the false smile and false voice off his mother's face. The son would like: just once, to hear his mother's smile, her voice.

And there's this:

The father's name fits into the mother's mouth. The father's name fills the mother's mouth completely. No is a word that does not fit into the mother's mouth. She tears off its head and feet but it still doesn't sit quite right.

The son takes the mother's hands. The son's wish: to cut the father's name out of the mother's mouth and make room for lots of other words. He would like: just once, to hear the mother's mouth speaking without the father.

eleven

The son tucks his lower lip under his teeth. Eiske is lying on the bed in the son's room; the floor creaks under the son's feet. Eiske is on the bed, eating gooseberries, only the unripe ones. Green berries pop; Eiske is eating with her mouth open.

The son wraps his lips around Eiske's head and Eiske says *Iloveyou*. The son thinks of Marie, thinks of her face; he pulls Marie's face over Eiske's head and says: *Iloveyoutobits*.

You're going to kill your father; you can't help it, Eiske says later and crams a handful of green berries between her teeth; they taste sour, like Eiske's words, and the son gets up and leaves in silence.

twelve

It has to be this way, says Eiske.

Foryouforyouforyou, says Eiske.

Then she folds her lips inwards, the way you tuck the sleeves of a sweater under, and speaks outside-in, into her belly where the worms and apples and gooseberries are. The son doesn't know what Eiske's saying, and even if he did, he'd say: I don't know what Eiske has up her sleeve.

What lies between the waistband and the hem of a T-shirt is kept very quiet, says Eiske and unbuttons her jeans, her long fingernails on the metal of her belt.

Keeping things quiet is the language the neighbours speak. This was a foreign language for the mother when she first arrived, with her oversized hats that cast three-quarters of her face in shadow, and her dresses that swept the gravel. Keeping things quiet is a loud language—the mother could hear it three houses away, on the street, through the walls. She learned the language quickly, if a little inaccurately.

Silence is now the mother's language.

The mother tongue is quiet, a difficult language for the son; he fails to learn it.

thirteen

Eiske is leaning against the window in the son's room, her hands stroking her breasts, her belly, her thighs; she moves her hand back and forth between her legs. She has her eyes closed, her mouth slightly open, and she takes short, sharp breaths in time with her hand.

The son hears nothing. He senses her hand touching her labia. When Eiske notices the son, she puts her hands up, places them on her head. *Now I'm not Marie any more*, she says, and throws the father's cut-out name at the son.

The blood is drying, flaking, on her hands. And in the son's mouth.

fourteen

The son shoves his hands into his pockets when the father's coffin is carried down the steps. There are six coffin-bearers; six men in black trousers and shirts, and the coffin is also black and shiny, like the body of a dead beetle in the dirt. The coffin is an animal; the animal has six legs, which are men.

One of them has a stoop.

None of them is crying.

fifteen

They're all sitting at the kitchen table. All means the son and the mother and Eiske.

People rarely keep quiet about things that have been kept quiet, and they're no good at it, says Eiske.

They compare the size of their hands; one size is missing. Your hands are big, the biggest of all, says the mother to the son. It's a reproach and a relief.

They sit there until night comes. They don't know what to do with the night. No longer does the night belong to the father. They speak very little. They means the mother and the son.

Speaking is Eiske's language.

Soon, says Eiske, *soon everything will be all right.*

And both of them, the mother and the son, have to repeat these words, over and over, until the night swallows up the son's hands and the way the mother looks at them.

lisa and elias and me

Elias didn't try to kiss me — maybe he has a girlfriend after all,
Lisa says at school on Monday, during break. She's holding
an apple. *Nonsense, 'course he doesn't,* I say, and Lisa sighs
a little and says, *I wonder if Elias thinks I'm pretty — what
do you think?* Everyone thinks Lisa's pretty, therefore Lisa is
pretty. I don't say that; I say *Sure.* Then Lisa says *But what
if he has a girlfriend?* And I say again *Nonsense, 'course he
doesn't,* and Lisa takes a bite of her apple. A spurt of juice
lands on my cheek. *I want him to fall in love with me,* says
Lisa with a little laugh.

Sure, I say.

Elias is nineteen and older than Lisa but younger than me,
and Lisa and I first met Elias on a Friday. I highlighted the
day in blue in my diary, because Elias was wearing a blue
T-shirt.

I'm going for a smoke, are you coming? Elias put that question to Lisa, not to me; I'm not the kind of girl who gets
asked that kind of thing. Or so Elias said, a different time.

In general, I'm not the kind of girl who gets asked anything. I only get told things — *It's cold*, for instance, or *I'm
taking you back to my place today.* Elias is very tall, 1.91 metres,
and the kind of guy I used to want to marry one day. He's the
kind of guy who can only be loved; it's impossible to be in
love with him, because Elias isn't in love with anything either
and only loves — gin, for instance, or YouTube clips of *The Annoying Orange* or American English. But it doesn't really take
love or being in love to get married; it doesn't take anything

at all. That's what I think. Lisa thinks it takes both, and Elias wants to be at least thirty before he's the kind of guy who thinks one might need love, or to be in love, or to get married, or anything at all.

Come here, look! he smiles, at me. Lisa has a squeaky-duck voice and Elias is smiling, and when he's standing right in front of us, his eyes are looking at me but it's Lisa he's smiling at, because I'm not the kind of girl who gets smiled at either. Then he says *Will you dance with me?*, and because that's a question, it's for Lisa, as is the smile that goes with it; and all that's left for me on this particular evening is one leaning against the disco wall, one gin and tonic, and onetwothree Elias-glances over Lisa-shoulders.

Do you think he's fallen in love with me?, Lisa asks on Monday in school, and I say *Of course*, and Lisa throws her bottle of water up in the air, catches it in her right hand and laughs.

I was in Elias's room; we were sitting knee to knee, hip to hip, shoulder to shoulder, head to head, and his hand was on my knee.

I'm going to sleep with you now, Elias said, and I wanted to ask if I'm also the kind of girl you don't have to be romantic with, but: *You're not the kind of girl who gets answers, Ines.* Knee to kneehip to hipshoulder to shoulderhead to head we sat.

I would really like to tell Lisa about it, but she's my friend and she's in love with Elias.

Listen, Lisa's my friend and—

I can't find the words for the sentence. I can never find words for my sentences. When I woke up, Elias was gone. I fold the piece of paper that said *Gone shopping* into big and then small rectangles, my hair falling in my face. Elias puts the brown paper bag down on the worktop beside me; I fish out an orange; I like the way your fingernails turn orange when you peel one; and Elias jingles his bunch of keys, then hangs them on my big toe by the Peace key ring. Elias likes it when I sit on the kitchen worktop wearing nothing but shorts, my feet dangling.

Okay, if you want to — I don't know if you — Well, some-one needs to tell Lisa because — You're not the kind of girl who stays for breakfast, Elias says and takes my hand, and the tips of his fingers touch mine. I look out the window. I'm not that kind of girl. There's no saying it, but Elias doesn't un-derstand, because I'm not the kind of girl who gets answers, and so he just lifts the lid of the bin so that I can throw the orange peel in.

Lisa is sometimes right and sometimes not. And the first sometimes usually outnumbers the second sometimes. *Hey, maybe Elias doesn't have a girlfriend . . . I got a text from him — What you doing today? Coming to my place? — We're texting each other now, you know.*

Yeah, I say.

Aha, I say.

Good, I say.

I don't want Lisa to be sitting on the worktop in Elias's kitchen, between the fridge and the sink, or on the window ledge looking out at the world, because that would be like taking a book and tearing out the first page and the last and a random page in between. *It's not like that*, says Elias, be-cause Elias doesn't read books, but Elias says a lot and most of it isn't true.

I'm really nervous; I don't think Elias is the kind of guy you can be nervous around.

Sure you can, I say. *Or maybe he really is that kind of guy*, I add and bite my tongue before I can say the kitchen belongs to me. But what use is a tongue anyway? I'm not the kind of girl who needs a tongue; I'm not the kind of girl who has anything to say.

Lisa lives on the top floor and you can smoke in her flat. When I get married, I want a house and someone who not only laughs but also asks questions and smiles, smiles at me. I can hear the heavy steps that aren't Lisa's from outside her door, and I recognise the shoes in the hall.

Elias — Ines; Ines — Elias, says Lisa, and Elias and I have no choice but to nod and say hello and laugh. When Elias, Lisa and I stand next to each other, Elias is a good deal taller than me, and taller than Lisa.

Elias, you and Ines must have met before — do you remember? says Lisa, and because Lisa is the kind of girl who gets answers and gets smiled at, Elias does both: *Yes*, he says.

And because I'm the kind of girl who gets looked at, he does that, and sits down beside me on the sofa, but not knee to knee and —

In school on Monday a girl throws her water bottle up in the air and catches it with one hand, takes a bite out of an apple and sends a spurt of juice flying. The girl is pretty, Lisa is her name, and she has a boyfriend by the name of Elias. The thing about the names is: there's one more letter in Elias, an e more than there is in Lisa, and the girl laughs and sweeps back her hair, and Elias is the extension of Lisa and Lisa is there within Elias.

Elias is not the kind of guy who falls in love. He only loves, for instance.

Elias has fallen in love with me, says Lisa, and sometimes Lisa's right and sometimes she's not.

I'm happy for you both, I say.

And sometimes I lie and sometimes I don't.

what björn did not imagine

This is what Björn did not imagine in terms of breaking up: two black suitcases, several boxes, and a girlfriend, in this case Irina, creating gaps on the bookshelves and space in the drawers to the right-hand side of the bed. What he also did not imagine: this searching for words after all the silence and keeping quiet. No, Björn had imagined it loud, with much shouting, accusation-hurling, door-banging; had imagined he might go on a bit of a pub crawl, drink too much beer, and come back to find the flat Irina-less. The one thing he hadn't reckoned with was helping Irina with the packing.

Björn thought things would work out with a woman like Irina, that it'd last. It did last too, for a couple of years. Björn and Irina, Irina and Björn, that had a ring to it, it sounded good to Björn. At some point it no longer sounded good to Irina; she didn't say so, didn't say anything, in fact, just sat at the kitchen table and cried a bit, then a bit more; she wiped her smudged mascara and said I'm sorry. They had drifted apart, she said some time later, and they really shouldn't make too big a deal of it. The soggy, scrunched-up tissues landed in the bin.

So here's Björn, folding sheets and putting them in boxes that have *Shoes* and *Clothes* written on them in Irina's big, round hand; and here's Irina, walking past the same picture for the third time, until he takes it down and says *This one's yours, Irina.*

Have I got everything? Irina wonders and wanders through the rooms, puffing up her cheeks and blowing the air out. She gets to the kitchen eventually, looks at her suitcases and boxes, at the fruit bowl on the table, at Björn, then sits down beside him. She sighs and clears her throat, and Björn thinks of the way she sings when she's hoovering, and how her cheeks go red when she's cooking or baking. Björn wants to say *Irina*; to say *Stay*.

The hall, you haven't done the hall yet, says Björn and smiles; the smile is for Irina but she doesn't want it. He can hear her in the hall, opening drawers and removing her gloves and hats, taking her coats off the hooks; he hears the drawers banging shut, then a short silence. Björn imagines Irina looking in the mirror, her eyes tired, running a hand over her hair; he hears her sighing, her footsteps heading for the kitchen; she looks at one of the suitcases—just at the case, not at Björn; the zip hisses as she closes the case, its teeth snagging in a corner of woolly green hat.

Björn, says Irina, dragging a case out into the stairwell; Björn studies the open door. *I'm leaving now.* Her voice freezes. *Yeah. Yeah.* Björn studies Irina's chin. *Björn, I'm leaving now*, and Björn says *Uh-huh, okay*, and Irina leaves the case near the top of the stairs and puts her arms around Björn, on his shoulders, his back, his neck, but her arms don't belong there any more. He had not imagined Irina crying at the end. He keeps quiet, doesn't say *It's okay* or *Take care, okay?* or anything else ending in okay; he says *That's it then*, and Irina lugs her case down the stairs, its base thumping off the steps. Irina comes back for the boxes, and the second suitcase, and then the door downstairs closes.

Björn imagines Irina coming back, standing at the apartment door with her two black cases and her boxes and asking *May I come in?* Björn imagines this for two days and then the doorbell rings. Irina doesn't take her finger off the bell until he opens the door; she doesn't ask if she can come in, and she has no black cases or boxes with her, only a small white handbag and the key to Björn's apartment, which she hands to him; she doesn't say or ask anything, just turns on her heel, then there she is at the top of the stairs again, then—

Irina, he says. She turns around and looks at him with very big, very questioning eyes and a slight tilt to her head. Björn studies Irina's shoes, her hands, her cheek—

Listen, Björn, I've got to go.

Okay, he says, *I know, I just wanted to, I—when did you open that carton of milk?* Irina straightens her T-shirt and pushes herself off the banister. *The day before yesterday*, she says, and Björn would like to put his arms around Irina, to hold her tight, and Irina gives Björn a quick nod, and then she's gone.

how we forgive

I

Wencke. Eighty-seven. Wrinkled hands. Overstretched Achilles tendon. High cheekbones. Wencke. Dead mother.

II

To my mind, people consist of hands, Achilles tendons and cheekbones; whatever is underneath can be concealed by ropes most days and hung by them on others. The latter are tar days, days like today.

Why is the sun shining, I ask, addressing no one, for there's no one there you could ask such a question.

My voice is cold and wet like the earth which is being flattened by my shoes and the others' shoes, all our shoes. Maybe I'll snip the eyes and mouths out of our faces and bury them, maybe I'll pull the Achilles tendons out of our heels—this is what I feel like saying but it would not be dramatic enough; so I just stick the *Sorryforyourloss* looks to my eyelids and tape my mouth shut with the *Howareyou* lines. Then I proceed with the others, my eyes and mouth shut, to the graveyard to bury the mother.

Death seldom comes alone, I say. *That is not something to keep quiet about*, I say. I don't say it to anyone, for there's no one there to whom you could say such a thing.

My feet are pressing down, squashing the earth flat that others are breaking up, digging up to make room for a coffin, as if it were irrelevant whose coffin.

III

What lies between the hands, the Achilles tendon and the cheekbones is foodstuff. They have thrown this food into a coffin, a white one. There is nothing nice, nothing amusing about the whiteness of this coffin under the brown clay, to the strains of Schubert's black Symphony in B minor. They chucked the food in the coffin, and the coffin in the dug-up earth. *What's behind the handsAchillestendoncheekbones is what is missing in the food.* I say this out loud and in squares and the others cry and the tissues tremble in their hands like the tulips they toss on the sutured earth.

People should not cry over the food, I think to myself, and remain silent. My hands fold the unused tissue, and back home in the living room I bite the heads off the tulip stems and eat them behind closed curtains.

IV

The way hair is slicked and combed by the rain, the words I serve up are combed and brushed on plates that have as many edges as my mother's voice. The others savage and gobble and gulp the words, wolfing them down like meat, their jaws grindinggrindinggrinding.

Why are you eating, I want to ask, but there is no one who would answer; they are tearing the meat with their teeth, grinding their teeth and the words between them, behind them, never in front.

You hear stories about people going to the dogs for no reason, I say. *That's the saddest thing ever.*

People always look their best when they're dying, they all said, and they were all wrong.

My mother's hands, Achilles tendons and cheekbones

did not look good when she was dying. And what lay behind them never looked good, but no one wants to hear that, or to hear how ropes could never hang it, how red-veined hands left red prints on cheeks, how the cheekbones screamed and the Achilles tendon sobbed as she ran — away and far and far away. And the others just turn their heads.

When someone has died, it doesn't matter what they were like or who they were, only that they are no more, that they're dead and that tears must be shed. *When someone has died, we must forgive*, the others say. *No*, I say and think of my mother's hands, which are big and gnarled, with long fingernails. That woman can hit like a man, the others used to say, and now they are silent.

Wencke, the others say, and in their mouths the name tastes of butter and bunches of flowers, of blue skies and blackberries.

Wencke. I scream, I sob, I punch the air. *Wencke*. I scream the name, I sob it, I punch it into the air. *Wencke*. I pronounce the name the way my mother was.

V

The phrases I utter are the kind I'm told are usually said on days like this. We pray, we stand, we wait, weep, walk and eat as if we were doing it for the first time, which is not at all fitting for my mother. My mother was a woman who never did anything for the first time, and if she did, she never let it show.

To Wencke, someone says and glasses clink; I feel like shattering them the way my mother could shatter my laughter.

I feel like: grabbing the glasses, smashing them and

screaming and using the shards to cut the others' cheek-bones from their faces, their hands from their arms and their Achilles tendons from their heels.

I also feel like: digging up the floor and piling all the cheekbones, hands and Achilles tendons in together.

And then: they can all cry as if for the first time.

To Wencke, the someone says and the glasses clink and I neither smash nor scream nor cut; I say *To Wencke*.

The phrases I utter are the kind I'm told are usually said on days like this.

VI

I am trying to write a story about my mother, who goes to the dogs for no reason. I can't seem to get beyond this first sentence.

The moment feels like a run-over cat. My mother is the cat; the newspaper says *87-year-old woman killed in car crash*; I fold the paper over and see my mother's face. There were two people in the car, my mother and someone else. The some-one else was me. I turned the key, released the clutch slowly, the car purred like the dead cat. Before I hit the accelerator, I opened the passenger door and let death in and myself out.

VII

I stuff my hands into my pockets as the coffin is carried down the steps. My fingernails are bitten to the quick; between my hips and my neck an opaque blister has developed, and in it are my mother's hands, which I detached from her arms and ate; my mother's cheekbones and Achilles tendons are in there as well. I can't burst the blister open as it's made of stone; that doesn't matter — the fingers are mine now.

The men are carrying the coffin, seven of them; it had to be seven because I wanted it that way. Some say a cat has the equivalent of seven human lives, and one of them was my mother's. The coffin is maggoty white. In the restaurant later, when it's dark, the men's coats on the window ledges look like rolled-up dead kittens.

VIII

To my mind, people consist of hands, Achilles tendons and cheekbones; whatever is underneath can be concealed by ropes most days, and hung by them on others. The former are days like today.

I sever my hands at the wrists, cut the cheekbones out of my face and pull the Achilles tendons out of my heels. I have two sets of each already, since my mother died.

Does anyone still write stories in which people forgive for no reason, I write. I get beyond this first sentence:

Wencke. Eighty-seven. Wencke. My dead mother.

translator's note

Did you know that the Alpine salamander (*salamandra atra*) — a small, shiny, lizard-like creature an Austrian might encounter on a mountain hike — has a gestation period of up to three years? The higher the altitude of its habitat, the longer the gestation period. It is a wondrous thing that a creature so small can take such a long time to gestate; it is a comforting thing too, especially for anyone working in the creative arts, where gestation periods frequently exceed those of the largest mammals and the smallest amphibians, regardless of habitat.

It would not be improbable to find an Alpine salamander in the tender, thorny, disturbing and beautiful world of Nadja Spiegel's writing. But I'm not going to discuss the stories here; instead, I am going to tell you a bit about this collection's gestation in English. In doing so, I hope to contribute to the bigger picture of how "foreign fiction" makes it through the AnglophonTex barrier.

I am shamelessly mixing metaphors now, as Anglophon-Tex (trademark pending) is more like a breathable waterproof membrane than a birth control device. This invisible membrane keeps out all but a tiny percentage of literature written in languages other than English, while literature written in English can escape readily into other world languages. Permeating this barrier from the outside takes patience, passion and perseverance — but this book has made it through, thanks to a brave publisher and many others who helped along the way.

This project was conceived in 2011, which would make the gestation four years; but strictly speaking, Dalkey Archive

Press didn't get involved until 2012, which makes it more like the Alpine salamander's three years. It went like this:

In late 2011, Karin Fichtinger-Grohe, the dynamic Minister, Counsellor and Deputy Head of Mission at the Austrian Embassy in Dublin at the time, asked me to read Nadja Spiegel's stories and to help her select one to represent Austria in Dublin's first ever European Literature Night event, "Words on the Street." This was scheduled for May 2012. We shortlisted our favourite stories from the collection, bearing in mind that the story would be read aloud and should be approximately fifteen minutes long. We decided on "death and ophelia," and I was commissioned to translate it. I hadn't heard of Nadja Spiegel at the time, although she had already won several awards for young writers in Austria, both for poems and spoken-word performances. This collection, *manchmal lüge ich und manchmal nicht*, had been published earlier in 2011 by Skarabaeus, a literary imprint of Austrian publisher Studienverlag. It was Nadja's first book-length publication and it had been garnering great praise in the Austrian media and beyond.

I immediately liked Nadja's poetic, playful and imaginative style. It reminded me of something I'd heard Irish writer Éilís Ní Dhuibhne say about the modern short story, that it is more poetic than the novel, more suggestive, dealing more in metaphor and symbolism. Ní Dhuibhne believes that natural short story writers combine the sensibilities of poets with those of novelists, and I believe that this is very true of Nadja Spiegel.

Apart from the translation challenges Nadja's writing posed, which I enjoyed, there was a slight typographical challenge: the original edition is all in lowercase letters, not a capital in sight. In German, which uses a lot more capitals than English, some writers make an aesthetic statement by adopting an all-lowercase style in their prose; in English, this trend is more common in poetry than prose, but at least in poetry the line breaks give visual cues. Long passages of lowercase prose in English can be very difficult to read, with no capitals to announce new sentences or proper names. The "caps or no caps" dilemma was largely irrelevant for the acoustic "Words on the Street" event, but it came up again on the next leg of the translation journey.

The next stage was to find a publisher for the whole collection in English. As luck would have it, I'd had a couple of meetings in Dublin with John O'Brien of Dalkey Archive Press, who had previously selected a short story I'd translated by a different Austrian author for inclusion in the *Best European Fiction* anthology. I introduced John O'Brien to Karin Fichtinger-Grohe from the Austrian embassy, and we talked about everything from translation, to Austrian writers, to Austrian wine. John was very open to seeing a sample of Nadja Spiegel's work, and we also arranged a meeting and dinner while she was in Dublin. There is no doubt that ideas have a better chance of hatching when people meet in physical as well as online environments.

The people at Dalkey Archive Press were impressed with Nadja and with sample translations I provided, so they contacted her publisher and proceeded to negotiate a rights deal. For reasons beyond a translator's ken, this took a very long time, though apparently it often does.

In the meantime, I heard that *The Stinging Fly*, an Irish literary journal which has showcased some of the best of Irish short fiction and poetry over the years, was planning a special translation issue for summer 2013 and looking for submissions. I submitted two stories by two different authors, one of which was Nadja's "death and ophelia." The journal accepted this story for publication. There was a lot of to-ing and fro-ing about who held the English-language rights, as the contract between Dalkey Archive Press and Skarabaeus / Studienverlag hadn't yet been signed off by both parties, but it all worked out in the end. The story was published all-lowercase, reflecting the original edition. While the feedback was positive in terms of the story itself, a number of people said they found the total lack of capitals a barrier to enjoying it. I reported the feedback and asked Nadja if she'd mind, for the book publication, if we went with conventional caps for the body text, to which she agreed. As a nod to Nadja's no-caps style in German — and because we think it suits the book anyway — we have styled the book's cover and the titles of the individual stories all lowercase. Just in case you were wondering . . .

Between the jigs and the reels, it was June 2014 before the paperwork for my contract to translate the book was signed off, but then it was full steam ahead. Nadja was very patient and helpful when I had queries about linguistic nuances or details I couldn't find answers to elsewhere (Was it a mountain lake if it tasted salty? Is this passage a flashback or when did Meta and Paul become lovers? Was it the green pine tips or the pine cones they ate during the war?).

I handed up my translation on 20 December 2014 and it went into editing and production after that. I was nervous about the editing process, because if you're translating writing that is quite experimental and poetic, you're never quite sure if it comes across in English. Getting a friend's or a loved one's seal of approval is not the same as that of a professional editor. Also — what if they want to "smooth out" some of the deliberately unconventional imagery or collocations? What if they want to impose strict punctuation rules on sentences that are often more stream of consciousness? Thankfully, Frances Riddle and Jeff Higgins at Dalkey Archive Press were very enthusiastic about the stories and had only a few questions and suggestions, all of which were very pertinent.

The following people deserve my particular thanks for making this book happen: first and foremost, the author, Nadja Spiegel; John O'Brien and all at Dalkey Archive Press; Anna Stock, Dorothea Zanon and Georg Hasibeder at Skarabaeus / Studienverlag; Karin Fichtinger-Grohe of the Austrian Foreign Ministry; all the funding bodies who have supported this publication; Jane Alger and the "Words on the Street" team at Dublin UNESCO City of Literature; Declan Meade of *The Stinging Fly* and Nora Mahony, co-editor of the 2013 translation issue; Monika Schlenger, retired librarian and champion of literary translation at Goethe-Institut Irland; my colleagues from the Literary Translation Lab, who provided critical feedback; my No. 1 Fan, Fiacc O Brolchain; and many more who offered encouragement.

Finally, thanks to all you readers who have found this particular Alpine salamander. Please enjoy it and tell your friends about it!

Rachel McNicholl
Dublin, April 2015

Nadja Spiegel, born in 1992 in Dornbirn (Vorarlberg, Austria), has been writing since she was eleven years old. She has won several prizes for her writing: the Meta-Merz-Preis (for poets under age 24) in 2009; the audience award at the World Water Day literature competition in Bregenz in 2010; *Sprichcode 05*, a competition run by the city of Leonding in upper Austria, in 2010; and the exil-literaturpreis (young writers category), Vienna, 2011.

Since 2008 Nadja's work has been published in anthologies and in literary magazines including *Die Lichtungen*, *Miromente* and *Kolik*. Her first prose collection *manchmal lüge ich und manchmal nicht* (*sometimes i lie and sometimes i don't*) was published by Skarabaeus Verlag (Austria) in 2011. The story "death and ophelia" from that collection, translated by Rachel McNicholl, was selected to represent Austria in "Words on the Street", Dublin's first European Literature Night, in May 2012. The story was subsequently printed in a special translation issue of Irish literary magazine *The Stinging Fly* in summer 2013.

Spiegel has appeared at festivals and literature forums in Austria, Germany and Ireland. In November 2014, her play *kilometerfressen macht auch nicht satt* (*eating up the miles won't fill you either*) was premiered in Theater Kosmos, Bregenz, Austria. The play is based on some of the stories in *sometimes i lie and sometimes i don't*.

Rachel McNicholl is a freelance translator based in Dublin, Ireland. She studied German, Italian and French for her BA, went on to do an MA in German literature, then side-stepped from research into publishing and journalism, where translation was always a big element of her work. She lived in Zurich and Hamburg before returning to Ireland. Apart from translating, she currently works as a freelance editor, a guest lecturer and an adult literacy tutor.